RUFUS

Son of Simon, Friend of God

LOREN PAUL DECKER

MEDITERRANEUM
Creta Insula
PENTAPOLIS
Barca
CYRENAICA
Labya
Berdoa

RUFUS

Son of Simon, Friend of God

LOREN PAUL DECKER

First Edition

NEWMAN SPRINGS PUBLISHING
320 Broad Street
Red Bank, NJ 07701

First originally published by Newman Springs Publishing 2021

Cover design by Jim Deering
RUFUS image—Vector Composite

Inside Front Cover Images
Ancient Jerusalem—Composite by Jim Deering
Ancient Cyrene map Black & White—Public Domain
Via Dolorosa—Fr. Vester, Jerusalem, Public Domain

ISBN 978-1-63692-225-6 (Paperback)
ISBN 978-1-63692-226-3 (Digital)

Printed in the United States of America

Endorsements

Nearly two thousand years ago, a letter was written by the Apostle Paul. Today, that very same letter is known as the Book of Romans, or the Letter to the Romans, in the Bible. The letter contained advice, encouragement, and, near the end, personal greetings to Paul's dearest friends. Some of them were described as hard-working, others as having found approval in various circles, and still others as beloved family and relatives. But one friend stands out. He was "chosen by God", and no one else is described quite like that. Who was this man? He is called Rufus, and his story is one that must be told today. Blending history, research and story-telling, this book will bring Rufus to life, and will fuse that ancient letter with our world today.

—Ellyn Bouts

Loren's powerful writing brings his characters vividly to life and ushers the readers effortlessly into their world. "Rufus" is a rich, captivating adventure that you won't forget!

—Randy Stonehill
One of the pioneers of contemporary Christian Music

"Rufus" is a compelling novel of what was and what may have been. Loren Decker skillfully brings biblical characters to life. I was moved to tears.

—Mary Carberry, M.Ed.

The Scriptures are full of names because the Gospel of Jesus Christ changes real people. Rufus is an imaginative attempt to explore the backstory of God's gracious workings in the life of one such person. Loren Decker weaves fixed points of history and the biblical narrative into the story of a young man who experiences God's transformative forgiveness. May God use Decker's novel to remind us not to pass over the many names in Scripture lightly, but to rejoice in God's salvation of countless men and women whose names are written in the Book of Life.

—Peter Murdy
Former Pastor of First Congregational Church, Middleboro, Mass.

Loren Decker brings to life the story of Rufus of Cyrene where we witness the transforming power of Jesus' sacrificial love in His life and those around Him. Decker's writing puts flesh and blood, heart and soul into his characters and compels us to feel their joy, sorrow and pain. This novel whets the appetite to again explore the truth of the gospel.

—Terri Ellis
Member, King's Baptist Church, Vero Beach, Florida

Loren takes a little mentioned character of the Bible and weaves an imaginative tale of what might have been. A fun read, but one filled with redemption and forgiveness, the foundational way of others to see Christ in us.

—Bob McCaw
Longtime friend

The story of Rufus is the story of a young man who admired his father. Were it to be written, my own life story would track on a similar path. My dad was a simple preacher who truly believed the message of the Gospel. To this day, decades after his passing, I continue to admire his faith and his spirit. Reverend Stanley Decker carried the cross with strength and humility. He was a wonderful father... and I shall see him again someday, in the Land of the Living. Until then, this book is dedicated to his memory.

CONTENTS

FOREWORD

Loren delicately weaves fiction with tradition and biblical truth. He imaginatively teases out the human narrative of the first century—the conversations that may have been, the scenes that may have unfurled, the emotions and the questions, and the unforgettable soothing interaction of Christ with His Creation.

Decker's work is altogether symmetrical. At pivotal moments, thick in the heart of the story, he guides us to the voice of Christ singing David's Psalms. Then that same melodic voice sings to us in the closing. He interlaces the human tragedy—a crippled boy waiting at the docks for his father who'd never return—with Jesus's abounding love speaking to each of us so uniquely. Years later, that blind boy is finally met, walks arm in arm, with Jesus, his Abba.

Loren Decker uses minimal space to remind us of the stark truth about Jesus: even the briefest of encounters with Christ, like Rufus had, leads to a life that is forever changed!

—Gregory Kelley, UK

ACKNOWLEDGMENTS

Thank you, Jim, for the many hours of editing, the guidance, and the love. You helped me turn a concept in my head into a story from my heart.

Thank you to my family for the encouragement and the patience you displayed while I sat at the kitchen counter with my laptop. Amanda, thank you especially for the exhortation to keep writing. I love you.

Thank you to the family at LifeHouse Church. You all inspire me with your love for God and one another. A special thank you to my proofreaders, Madeline, Karen, and Greg.

Also, thank you to Brian Hardin from the Daily Audio Bible for deepening my love for the Scriptures as we gather daily "around the global campfire."

A heartfelt thank you to Quinton Bowen for catching the vision of Rufus artistically and putting it on paper with a pen, an ink, and a wonderful skill. Q, you have a great gift.

Thank you to my staff at LifeHouse who make it possible for me to write—Allie, Kevin, Scotty, Jaqueline ("Little Rock"), Pastor Mike, Pastor Sandra, and our wonderful team of elders.

Lastly, bless you, Jack and Diane, for your love and friendship over the years.

Introduction to Rufus

As the Apostle Paul closes the New Testament book of Romans, which is his letter to the church in Rome, he offers personal greetings to a number of people who are special to him. One of those mentioned is Rufus, whom Paul describes as "having been chosen by the Lord to be His very own." Paul adds that Rufus's mother had been like a mother to him as well. Just who was this man, Rufus, and in what manner did Jesus choose him? We have our first clue in the Gospel of Mark when we are told that Simon of Cyrene, who was forced to carry the cross for Christ on the tortuous road to Golgotha, was the father of Rufus.

Tradition states that Mark wrote his gospel (the second book of the New Testament) while living in Rome, so it is likely that he mentions Rufus because he was a well-known leader of the persecuted church there, some thirty years after Calvary. A logical trail leads us to that conclusion. The book of Acts mentions that men from Cyrene were present at Pentecost, listening to Peter preach and hearing the words in their own language. Some three thousand converts were added to the church that day.

Later, during the persecution of Christians in Jerusalem, certain men from Cyrene, most likely Rufus among them, escaped to Antioch and helped establish the church there. The newly converted Saul, now Paul, spent a full year ministering in Antioch, likely the time period when he became well acquainted with Rufus and his mother. From there, their next stop was probably Rome where they became pillars of the early church.

Taking these clues from Scripture, I have endeavored to bring Rufus to life. Though fiction, this story of the young Cyrenian is based on the Bible. Follow along as we accompany Rufus from his home in Northern Africa to Jerusalem and beyond. Perhaps we will come to see why he was selected by Jesus to be His very own.

Throughout this book, there will be sections inserted and a secondary storyline will appear. These behind-the-scenes subplots flesh out the people and places that existed concurrently with the life and experiences of Rufus.

CYRENE

Thomas of Thera

"An audible groan passed through the crowd."

Thomas of Thera lay writhing on the ground, a huge wooden mallet buried deep in his forehead. Blood pooled where he lay as he gasped for his last breath in the hot sun. His challenger and ultimate victor, the mighty Egyptian known as Ptolmine of Cairo raised his arms high in celebration, then retrieved his wooden weapon and delivered one last crushing blow to the fallen Thomas. An audible groan passed through the thousands of transfixed spectators.

The boisterous crowd had gathered to witness the savage sport of gladiator combat that day. Powerful men from Africa, Asia, and Europe came to the historic open-air coliseum to seek their fortune in battle, lethal conquests that paid their winners handsomely.

Rufus, my older brother, son of our father, Simon of Cyrene, had seen enough. As a fifteen-year-old boy, Rufus usually stayed until the end of the last match, but today was to be an exception.

Thomas of Thera was idolized by young Rufus. He had even met him once in our father's bakeshop. Now, Thomas was surely dead. Rufus ran as fast as his legs could carry him, his sandaled feet pounding the pavestones that led to the city's center section and the bakery. I was on the wide sidewalk of the main marketplace, just outside the shop with Father when we saw Rufus running toward us. We could clearly see the distraught look on his face.

"What is troubling you, Rufus?" father asked as he put down the bowl he held and wiped the flour from his hands.

I stood behind our father and peered at Rufus. I could see the concern in his eyes. I was a shy boy and deemed to be too young to watch the bloody games in the arena, but I knew something terrible had occurred. Out of breath, Rufus flung himself into Father's waiting arms and buried his head in his chest.

"The Egyptian killed Thomas!" Rufus exclaimed through gasps that shook his entire frame. "I saw it happen."

At that, he could hold it in no longer and burst into tears. Father pulled him close and spoke lovingly to his oldest boy. "Thomas was a hero to you, I know. But even heroes must die, my son. It is a hard truth to accept, but you are now almost a man yourself. You must learn the things a man knows, and that means understanding that death comes to us all."

"I thought Thomas would win today," Rufus moaned and collapsed into the chair by the doorway.

"No one can defeat the final enemy. Death is as sure as each sunrise." Our father rejected formal religion but was full of homespun wisdom and often relied on adages from philosophers and poets to fit whatever situation was at hand. "Perhaps you should take a respite from the fight games in the coliseum. They are bloody and violent. You could do well to help me more here at the bakery."

Just then the street began to fill up with the crowd coming from the arena.

"Now would be a good time to start," said Simon. "This coliseum crowd looks hungry!"

The seaside arena had no shortage of willing contestants, and many of them had loyal followers who came in great numbers to cheer them on. Attendees placed large bets on the projected outcome of each battle. Depending on the skill and stamina of the opponents, contests could last for only minutes or for many hours. Oddsmakers were stationed in booths along the entranceway to the venue, where names were drawn for the day's pairings, and wagers were made based on the calculated advantages of a contestant's height, weight, quickness, and agility. Business was good.

Carved into the natural slope of a hillside that overlooked the shores of the shining sea, the open-air arena featured stone bench seating for the general public and high wooden porches for the wealthy guests. These "privileged platforms" featured comfortable lounge chairs under banners and canopies that fluttered against the deep blue Mediterranean sky. Built by the Greeks more than two centuries before, the arena was considered an architectural marvel. It was an acoustic masterpiece as well. It was not uncommon, during a theatrical performance, to hear the whispered voice of the off-stage prompter even if you were seated at the rear of the coliseum. The Greeks had used the outdoor venue for plays and political rallies. The famed scholar Socrates was said to have visited the coliseum. It was supposed that he was in attendance for a theater presentation written by one of his students. During one of the scheduled intermissions, he was urged by the crowd to speak. Tradition stated that he willingly ascended the stage and delivered a spontaneous and beautiful lecture on the Grecian philosophy of life and the arts.

The Roman influence of more recent years changed little of the ancient stadium's structure, but it did introduce the gladiator fights that were, more often than not, battles to the death. These days, the only whispered words heard in the arena were the pitiful pleas for mercy from fallen warriors. The crowd noise, on the other hand, was deafening.

My name is Alexander. I am a true believer today because of one incredible person whose life changed mine forever. He lived his life within the strong bonds of faith. These ties of trust held him securely. I, on the other hand, was someone who was less secure. I was safe enough in his shadow for he was my older brother. But on my own, I felt anything but safe.

This is not my story. It is his... He lived it. Every detail I will share with you is true. I saw much of it with my own eyes. However, it was my spiritual eyes that were slow to open to this truth I am writing about. What I saw as a boy perplexed me enough to close my spiritual sight for years. It was only then that love and forgiveness came to me arm in arm, but I am getting ahead of myself. I shall begin at the beginning and tell you the story of Rufus.

***

Cyrene was a teeming region on the northwestern tip of Africa. Its terrain was as varied as its people. The seaports along the Mediterranean were a sharp contrast to the desert lands to the south. Seafarers lived along the coastal territory while shepherds and farmers were abundant in the southern sector. Cyrene had been settled primarily by refugees from Thera, an island in the Aegean Sea, which was discovered by Spartans searching for a strategic outpost for their military. Thera, as history recorded, underwent a severe seven-year drought that sent its inhabitants packing. Many found the shores of Cyrene to their liking and never departed. Thus, the culture of Greece made its way to Africa and flourished in the Cyrenian region. It remained part of the empire of Alexander the Great, Plato, and Socrates for more than six hundred years. However, with the fading influence of Greece across the civilized world, Rome had methodically taken control of the weakened empire. Nearly a century ago Cyrene, like other nations, came under the rule of the Caesars.

Cyrene was home for Simon and our family. The marketplace where he worked was at the bustling center of life in the metropolis.

The Roman rule proved to be profitable for business, mostly due to the construction of roadways and the development of a busy seaport at Apollonia on the northern coast. Still, the citizens of Cyrene were fiercely independent, and they considered themselves a free state—not a Roman colony.

Simon had been a fixture in the commerce of the city since he was a young man. His father had settled in Cyrene years before he was born. Our ancestors had not come from Thera as many of their fellow Cyrenians had. Simon's parents arrived on the northern shores of the African continent, having journeyed from their former home in Ethiopia. Simon's father, known as Caleb, was Jewish by religion and African by birth. His ancestors had embraced the faith of Father Abraham hundreds of years before when the Queen of Sheba brought the worship of Jehovah back from her pilgrimage to Jerusalem and the courts of King Solomon. So impressed was she with Solomon's wealth and wisdom that she converted to the worship of the Hebrew God.

Although Grandfather Caleb was a devout Jew, Simon, my father, had no mind for such labels.

"I will sell them my pastries when they come out of the synagogue," Simon would say. "That's my religious duty."

And sell them, he did. It became a local tradition for Jewish worshippers to go straight from the synagogue to Simon's bakery after the close of each weekday service. There the crowd would discuss the lessons of the rabbis and the politics of the day. Simon would always have a daily special: a kosher treat of his own creation that he would feature on the top shelf of his window display. So popular were these confections that Simon soon hung a new sign above his shop door, "Top Shelf Bakery." It didn't take long for the coliseum crowd to follow the religious patrons and make their own way to Simon's establishment after every one of the brutal gladiator battles. That was how Rufus met Thomas of Thera. The popular warrior had a sweet tooth and enjoyed the notoriety and the affection of the crowd that gathered at the eatery. Much to the baker's delight, even the non-Jewish citizens followed suit and gathered in the marketplace after leaving the temple of Zeus and the smaller but no less popular temple of Apollo. These houses of worship traced their roots to the founding Grecian fathers but were still a part of Cyrenian life and culture.

"They can worship at a brothel for all I care," Simon was known to say. "I would still gladly feed them my cakes and sweets. A man usually cares as much for his stomach as he does his soul." The Top Shelf Bakery was, indeed, where the crowd was headed on this late afternoon, pouring out of the coliseum and into the main street that ran through the center of the city.

Within a half hour, Simon had sold out of most of his breads and cakes. Rufus had filled many orders and had dutifully collected the coins from the sales. The money weighed down the pocket of his tunic. It felt good to have the responsibility for the day's earnings. The fact that his father trusted him to care for the income from all the sales made Rufus's heart soar with excitement and pride.

Business at the bakery was better than good. Simon was turning a profit that propelled him to the forefront of the business community of Cyrene. He added tables and chairs to the Top Shelf, but it was becoming clear that a bigger space was needed. Simon explored a few possible sites, but none seemed satisfactory for a busy bakeshop.

One summer evening, Rufus returned home from the Top Shelf with our father and me. It had been another busy day at the bakery, and the three of us were tired but cheerful. We were surprised to find Uncle Mathias, older brother of our mother, Cecile, waiting for us on the hammock that hung in the courtyard of our elegant home in Cyrene. We were always pleased to see our favorite uncle.

Uncle Mat was loud and funny and very wealthy, having amassed a fortune in the shipping business. Years before, he had run away from home as a boy seeking adventure. Through a stroke of good luck, he caught on with a sea captain who was in need of a cabin boy. Mathias was born for the sea, it seemed. He learned every job onboard the ship and became the right-hand man for the seafaring ship's owner. He never tired of the rolling waves or the salt spray and therefore spent most of his growing up years out on the open water. Mathias eventually was able to purchase his own boat, and his incredible knack for sailing caused him to be much in demand by merchants and dealers who found him to be fast, reliable, and fair. By the time he was twenty-one, he had a fleet of vessels that transported trade goods to Britannia to the north and in return, brought back precious tin from the deep, dark mines along the coast of that country. He also returned home after each voyage with a variety of valuable items for the people of the African continent to buy at over-market high prices. Tin was his most lucrative commodity, however. It was vital in the making of bronze, and the Mediterranean nations were craving that metal for swords and shields, javelin heads, and body armor. Mathias unloaded tons of tin from Britannia at the docks of Haifa and Joppa, and in turn, he loaded his pockets with payments of silver and gold from the eager traders who would sell off the metal at ridiculous prices.

Uncle Mat's favorite "partner" was a tiny monkey that perched on his shoulder. The small chimp was a source of fascination to both children and adults alike. Cico, the monkey, was happy to see Rufus and me. We loved to feed the clever creature as a reward for a trick or two, for which Cico gladly complied. He hopped from Mathias's shoulder and scampered to us. He quickly climbed up onto Rufus's back and began exploring pockets in search of a treat. The trio of Simon, Rufus, and I laughed heartily at the antics of little Cico. Rufus managed to produce a breadstick from his bag. Quickly the monkey grabbed the small loaf and disappeared high in a cypress tree, where his chatter was testament as to how he felt about the still-warm bread.

"Even monkeys like your baked goods, Simon," said Uncle Mat. "Everyone does," he continued. "And that's what I came to discuss with you, my brother-in-law."

"Come in then," Simon replied. "Cecile will have supper ready for us, and we can talk over a meal."

"I've been sniffing around the kitchen, and I can't wait to find out what smells so good," Mathias said with a hearty grin. "My sister is as good a cook as you, Simon."

"No doubt about it," said Simon as the four entered the house.

Little Cico scrambled down from his perch and followed the hungry men into the home. As we sat down around the table, we could hear Mother shooing the monkey away from the kitchen.

"We will eat in a moment," she called, "if Cico doesn't beat us to it."

Rufus loved these nights. His uncle always had stories to share from his travels. Long after the food was eaten, our family would be in rapt attention as Mathias told of faraway lands and the people who lived in such places. He had most recently traveled to Israel. He spent several months in the land, uncovering the history and beauty of the special region. From Galilee to Jerusalem, Uncle Mat traversed the countryside and harbors, taking in the sights and culture of the Jewish nation.

"While there, I heard a man speak like none other I have heard before," said Mathias in a mysterious tone. "He not only talked like an angel, but he did something I cannot comprehend, nor can I ever forget. He fed a crowd of more than five thousand people with only a few fish and some loaves of bread. It occurred on the shores of Galilee. We had been sitting on the green grass of a hillside, and the hour was getting late. There were no eating establishments in the area, which I will get back to in a moment. The rabbi called out to the crowd and asked if anyone there had provisions. Just one small boy had a lunch basket, and in it were a few dried fish and some barley loaves. I cannot explain, but it became enough to feed everyone! With plenty left over… He just kept breaking off pieces, and when it appeared to run out, he suddenly had more… Had I not seen the miracle I wouldn't have believed it. But I was there and witnessed it. His name was Jesus of Nazareth."

Cecile had cleared the last of the supper dishes and had sat down again next to her husband. "Tell us more," she said softly to her brother.

"Well, I stayed close to this Jesus and his companions for a week or two, and from what I overheard, I can tell you what happened next. It went something like this… After the crowd was dismissed, the rabbi directed his disciples to go across the lake in a borrowed boat. They were none too happy to have to clean up after the impromptu feast, but Jesus insisted on it. As for him, he seemed exhausted and, apparently, he wanted some time alone. As I recall…"

***

Peter was the first one in the boat that evening. Grabbing the cord for the mainsail, he muttered, "The Master is really upset with us this time."

John, the second to board, echoed the sentiment. "He didn't even ask us to come and pray with Him," he observed. "I think He really wanted us to leave Him alone."

As the rest of the twelve climbed into the now crowded vessel, they got busy with the oars and cast off from the dock. It had been a long day. Now they faced the evening task of crossing the Galilean Sea.

Back on shore, Jesus watched them from a distance. He was tired. He was hungry. And He needed to pray. He climbed up a bluff and headed for the high cliff that overlooked the sea. It was there that He finally sat down and unpacked his satchel. Taking a deep breath, He let His body relax. He smiled when He pulled some bread from the leather bag. Holding it up to His mouth, He thought of the little boy who had brought this bread to the large green field where they had spent the day. It all began that morning with a spontaneous crowd begging to hear Him preach. He had obliged willingly; however, His disciples had resented the intrusion.

"Send them away!" they had demanded.

The band of twelve had been hoping for some downtime. They had many questions for the rabbi, and they were eager for answers. As long as there were crowds around, they knew their questions would have to wait. Now, after a particularly demanding week of ministry, they had finally convinced Jesus to come away for a private session, but when Sunday morning broke, they saw the throng headed for them. Jesus seemed to welcome them and spoke for hours while the Twelve had fumed on the edges of the crowd.

The grass on the hillside had been covered with a sea of blankets and makeshift canopies while the thousands listened to the wisdom and wit of Jesus. As the evening hours drew closer, a restlessness had overtaken most of the listeners. They were scrounging for food, but there was none. That's when the Twelve spoke up.

"You have got to send them home," said Thomas. "They all need to leave."

"No," Jesus had countered. "You feed them."

That produced a cynical laugh in Thomas's throat.

"Feed them what?" he queried. "Is it not obvious to you that we are miles from anywhere?"

Jesus looked patiently at His friends and simply said, "See what you can find."

Peter had been a little rough with the lad that he found was carrying lunch in his bag.

"Give it to me," he had barked.

Reluctant, the boy held on to his bread and fish.

"I'll bring it back in a few minutes," Peter said.

Turning to James, who was by his side, he grabbed the little basket from the boy's hands and said, "This is all the food there is. Run this to Jesus and prove there is nothing here for the crowd to eat. That should convince Him. Bring it back after He sees it. I'll stay here with the boy."

James cut through the throng and brought the little basket to Jesus who was just finishing a story from the Jewish Scriptures about a widow who was poor and needy. A prophet had asked her to pour out the little oil she had left into a cup—and a miracle had occurred.

"She just kept pouring." Jesus laughed. "She filled every vessel she could find."

Taking the basket from James, he turned back to the delighted group at his feet. "Here," he said. "Let me show you…"

He thanked His Father in heaven for the food and began passing it out to the hungry crowd. Each time He reached into the basket, more fish and bread came out. It did not stop until everyone had their fill. The Twelve had been ordered to serve and then clean up.

"Leftovers," said Jesus now as He tasted the bread He had saved in His bag.

The bread was sweet and made for a good supper for Him now. As He finished the last crumbs, He turned His attention to the sea.

The disciples' boat was barely visible through the gathering mist of evening. In the western sky, where the sun was setting, Jesus could clearly see a storm forming over the lake.

He was concerned about the Twelve. They had been so hesitant to serve lunch and had complained about cleaning up afterward. It seemed as though the miracle had been lost on them. But when the well-fed crowd began to call for Jesus to be their king, Peter and the others stood close to the Master, garnering as much of the attention and praise as they could.

"You are missing the point," Jesus had told them.

He had then sent them off with orders to meet Him next on the far side of the great lake.

Onboard the disciples' ship, all was in misery.

"We are going to get drenched," said Peter to his companions, and he nodded toward the western sky.

The storm had fully formed now and was to be on them soon.

"Perfect way to end a great day," said Judas cynically.

Night fell and with it came the rain. It poured out of the sky in torrents.

"Take down the sails before the wind takes them down for us!" Peter called from the stern.

The wind was blowing hard now as the disciples leaned into the oars and pulled against the gale.

"We are getting nowhere," moaned Peter.

About four hours later, they were still at their task. They had made little progress and were still far from the opposite shore. The storm raged on. A dread had overtaken them. It seemed as though Death itself was in the storm with jaws wide open wanting to swallow their ship.

"This is no normal night storm," one of the Twelve stated.

Everyone agreed and prayed for morning to arrive. They were soaked to the skin, they were exhausted, and they were plenty frightened.

Peter had stopped rowing when the rest noticed he was staring at the dark water. His mouth was open wide in apparent amazement.

"Grab your oar, Peter!" John had hollered. Peter did not move.

"Guys," Peter finally said, "a ghost just walked past the ship. I saw it."

No one doubted that this rough and tumble fisherman had just seen something. He was obviously uneasy. They all strained their eyes against the weather and darkness, looking for something…anything.

"There! Over starboard! What's that?" cried Matthew.

Peter stood and stared. Without a doubt, a lone figure stood thirty yards away, barely discernible in the dark rain but no doubt real.

"Name… Name yourself," Peter stammered. "Are you friend or foe?"

"Peter, it is I," the voice came across the open water.

"Jesus?" asked Peter, amazed.

"Yes" came the calm reply.

"But how…how…how can this be?" Peter was at a loss for any more words.

"Come to Me and see," Jesus called.

Quickly but gingerly, Peter swung his legs over the starboard side. He was battered by the strong wind and needed to hold on tight to the oarlock, lest he is blown over. He held his breath and jumped into the tempest-driven waves. But what was this? His feet hit the water as though hitting a solid rock. Peter didn't sink nor did he need to swim. He took a step, then another. He was walking. And as he neared Jesus, he could definitely recognize his friend, who was walking toward him, arms outstretched. Feeling more than a little confident now, Peter turned and looked back at the dumbfounded disciples.

"Look, guys," he called back to the boat, "I am walking on water!"

No sooner had the words escaped his mouth, he went down into the waves. Coming up coughing and gasping for air, the fisherman was barely managing to keep his nose above the stormy surface.

"Would you like a hand?" Jesus was leaning over him.

"Pull me up!" cried Peter.

Jesus extended his strong arm and pulled soggy Peter out of the water. Together they crossed the span of waves between them and the ship. Hands reached over the side and pulled the pair on board. As soon as Jesus stepped into the boat, the storm abated. Instantly. Gone. Ceased. And as they looked about in wonder, they found that they were at the dock on the western side of the lake.

"Who is this man who feeds many with little and stills the wind and waves?"

"Anyone for breakfast?" asked Jesus with a smile.

With the Twelve gathered around, He reached into his satchel and pulled out some leftovers.

"Pass it around," Jesus said after He had blessed it. "It's going to be another long day."

***

Uncle Mat stood up and went to the narrow archway that led out to the patio. He lit his pipe and slowly drew a cloud of sweet smoke into his lungs. It was clear that his purpose in sharing the story of Jesus and his disciples was about to be voiced. He took another deep pull on his pipe and exhaled slowly. After a pause, he continued telling of his time in Israel. "I later followed Jesus for several more weeks and saw him do many other amazing things. He healed a leper and caused a blind man to see. I have never before seen a man do such things as these. But more than any miraculous display, it was his words that stirred my heart. He could make you feel like heaven came down to earth and that life actually had meaning."

Our family was hanging on every word as Mathias continued his story.

"Back to the bread and fish miracle…" Mathias had a faraway look in his eyes as he spoke. "Right now, as we speak, every baker in Jerusalem is trying to capitalize on the 'miracle lunch,' as it is being called. Merchants by the score are selling 'Jesus miracle loaves' in the city and beyond. The leading religious establishment at the temple is pretty upset about it. They perceive Jesus to be a threat to their authority, but, Simon, I see this as a grand opportunity for you to open the best bakery in all the Mediterranean region. I will pay the costs if you will travel there with me and open a bakeshop in Jerusalem!"

Rufus could hardly believe his ears.

"Can we, Dad?" he heard himself say.

"Well, I know it sounds exciting, but this would require much planning," Simon cautioned his son. "Mathias, why don't we ponder an exploratory trip in a few months during Passover. We will test the market in Jerusalem."

Rufus
"He fell asleep with his racing mind full of images of fallen gladiators, miracle bread, and a rebel King named Jesus of Nazareth."

That night, Rufus could not sleep. He stared at the ceiling of his bedroom imagining distant Jerusalem. I was already fast asleep in the bed next to him for I was too young for such dreams of travel, but I learned the following day of the talk. Rufus listened to the night sounds outside his window…a jackal howling on the hill, a whisper of wind through the trees in the courtyard, an owl calling to its mate. Rufus would be sixteen years old in a few weeks. He would be a young man—no longer a boy. He felt different on this night, different than he ever had before. He remembered the coins in his cloak at the market and how responsible he felt working alongside his father. He decided that this was what it was like to be grown up.

Rufus climbed out of his bed and quietly went to the front of the house where he heard his uncle and father talking. He stood for a moment in the shadows and listened to their conversation. Uncle Mat was describing the political scene in Israel.

"The Romans are fed up with the religious leadership of the Jewish nation," Mathias said.

Rome was an occupying force, and Israel was a nation that was not free. The cultural climate was at a boiling point and the resistance against Caesar's military force was getting more and more organized.

"There is a move to make this Jesus of Nazareth the next king and take David's throne back by brute force," Rufus heard Mathias say. "The Zealots are talking up the incident with the loaves and fishes and the miracle feeding of the thousands. They claim that Jesus is a man of the people and that he would have the backing of the entire nation. They are recruiting Jewish supporters even now to come to Israel. One of my friends in the shipping industry named Joseph from Arimathea claims that there are a few in the Sanhedrin that would get behind such a move. He seems quite convinced that Jesus is the real deal. And he may have enough clout in the synagogue to back up his belief."

Both men knew what the Roman occupation meant. Although Cyrene thrived economically under Roman domination, Simon well knew the endless legalities and burdensome taxes he was responsible for as a resident of Cyrene. And both men understood that there was a growing sense of uneasiness amongst the Jewish community toward their Roman officials. Not unlike Jerusalem, Cyrene was also a clear example that occupied regions could not easily coexist with Rome. Not that many decades prior, the Jewish population of Cyrene had revolted against the Roman emperor, forcing the Roman military to come and attempt to suppress the uprising. Matters became out of hand as the Jewish resistance was stronger and more organized than Rome expected. The outbreak lasted two and a half years. Buildings were destroyed, and houses were burned. The Romans managed to quell the uprising by giving monetary concessions to the large

Zionist community, granting promises to pay for the rebuilding of the Cyrenian metropolis. Still, Rome was despised by the Jews, and an underlying tension permeated city life. The Jewish factions were waiting only for a leader to arise and free them of the oppressive tyranny of Rome. Both men were well aware of the renowned historical events of the Maccabean revolt and their short-lived success in holding the Seleucid empire at bay, not much more than a century before. The empire of Seleucus was built upon the land-grabbing successes of Alexander and was hell-bent on creating and maintaining a Grecian superstate. Jewish rebels, led by Judah Maccabees, resisted the takeover of their homeland, and for a time, they were successful in restoring Jerusalem to Hebrew hands.

"We need a Judah Maccabees here in Cyrene to oust the Romans," said Simon.

"Or a Jesus," said Mathias, only half-joking. "There is historical precedent for the weaker nation overthrowing the greater power." Simon was lost in thought and quiet for a time. "It is not unlike David versus Goliath." Despite the warm night, a shiver passed through Rufus's body.

"Perhaps we can entice the rabbi to make some miracle bread for our bakery," Simon said, grinning ear to ear.

"Dad?" Rufus burst back into the room and stood beside the lounge chair where his father was reclining.

"Rufus! You should be asleep by now." His father was stern.

"I wanted to tell you something," Rufus said earnestly.

"Be quick about it then, and get back to your room," Simon scolded.

"I just wanted to remind you that I am almost sixteen now, and I would be a great help on a trip to Israel. I will do everything you ask and more. Can I go with you? Please?"

Simon looked at his boy, so eager and earnest, so close to manhood. He scrunched up his forehead and sighed heavily. He knew that time was moving quickly and that indeed Rufus was getting to be a fine helper at the bakeshop.

"If I decide to go, I will take you with me," Simon finally said.

"Oh! Thank you, Father," Rufus gushed as he hugged Simon and then ran down the hallway to his bedroom.

"Alexander," he said before climbing back into bed, "help me to remember this night forever."

There, he fell asleep next to me, his racing mind full of images of fallen gladiators, miracle bread, and a rebel King named Jesus of Nazareth.

News from Jerusalem

Several weeks had passed since Uncle Mat's visit. Rufus spent much of his time at the Top Shelf, assisting his father and keeping an eye on me. He did not frequent the arena any longer. Since the death of Thomas, the sport had held little interest for Rufus. Something that did hold his interest was his birthday, coming in just a few days. To be sixteen in Cyrenian culture meant responsibility and learning. Rufus would soon enter the School of Higher Philosophical Thought, a learning center based on the teachings of Socrates. The Romans had not disbanded the school despite its Grecian foundation.

"Smart is smart, whether Greek, Roman, or Jew," the local saying went. "And Socrates surely was smart!"

Children did not receive formal early educational opportunities in Cyrene. However, at age sixteen, Rufus would be eligible to enter the school of Socratic thought. He couldn't wait for the start of his classes. Something inside him was restless though. "I'd rather gain knowledge through experience than to listen to what other men have concluded about the world we live in," Rufus told his mother one afternoon at the bakery.

Cecile often visited her husband's shop and sometimes took a turn in the kitchen. "You and the boys should take the afternoon off and go fishing," she would tell Simon. "You cannot work all the time!"

"But I need to work most of the time in order to keep you in the latest fashions," Simon would say with a merry laugh. Still, he would usually consent to his wife's urging and take the boys to their favorite fishing place at the shore for a few hours of relaxation and fun.

The day of his birthday finally arrived. As sixteen was an important milestone, many friends and neighbors came to celebrate. Rufus received many presents, and after finishing a grand dinner made by our mother, it was time to open them. Rufus unwrapped each gift and said his proper thank-yous. Uncle Mat gave Rufus a shaving kit from India, one that he had purchased while traveling in that distant land. It was a silver blade with an ivory handle and a matching mug and brush to go with it.

"You'll be needing that before long." Mathias chuckled.

Everyone laughed, except Cecile.

"He's growing up so fast as it is, brother. Next you'll be bringing a wife for him!" she said only partly in jest.

"It won't be long before he will think well of that notion too!"

Mathias ruffled the boy's hair and gave him a playful pat on the back. "Eh, Rufus?"

Uncle Mat was not known for his taste in women nor his success in relationships. He had been married several times, and each time the marriage had ended shortly after the honeymoon.

"My first love is the sea," he would say. "I am not cut out for domestic life."

Simon saved his gift for last. It was a rolled scroll, and as soon as Rufus opened it, he let out a whoop. It was a map of Jerusalem and a travel itinerary. It could only mean…

"We sail in two months' time," said his father with a smile.

Rufus hugged both parents, thanking them for the "best present ever!"

"Thank your father," mother remarked. "I was hesitant to let you go so far from home. Your father talked me into it."

Mathias jumped in. "I told your mother I would personally keep my eye on you," he said.

"That's what worries me the most," mother said.

"Fortunately, I won't have much time to worry about you, men," said Cecile. "I shall be running the Top Shelf Bakery back here at home. My sister is coming to help Alexander and me, and we have more than a few recipes to try out ourselves." I was delighted by the plan. Traveling to a foreign nation was not of much interest to me. Staying close to home sounded like a better option to my young ears.

A rousing cheer went across the courtyard of our home. Everyone, it seemed, shook hands with Simon and Rufus. Well wishes and congratulations were as numerous as the guests themselves as all who gathered now knew that Simon and Rufus were going to Jerusalem to open a Top Shelf Bakery in that beautiful city.

"Uncle Mat, are you really coming with us?" asked Rufus.

"Wouldn't let you go without me, lad," replied his uncle enthusiastically.

Another cheer went up from the crowd as uncle and nephew embraced.

***

The next morning, there was a buzz in the marketplace. Two travelers from Palestine had visited the Top Shelf Bakery and told the patrons what they had recently seen while in Bethany outside of Jerusalem. They were Jewish zealots, covering well-known areas of Jewish habitation in search of volunteers to help drive the Romans out of Israel. Much to Mathias's interest, they had recently been following the movements of Jesus of Nazareth. Rufus and Uncle Mat sat for an hour with the Israelites and listened to their accounts of the would-be king.

"He reportedly has raised three from the dead," said one zealot. "A woman from Nain has been on the temple record—testifying to the Sanhedrin that this Jesus raised her son from the dead. Also, there is a man in Bethany, our hometown, who was four days in the grave when the Nazarene called him forth. They say he walked out of the tomb, completely whole. We have talked to those who saw it occur!"

The other visitor spoke. "Most convincing to us is the claim of Jairus, a devout man of the synagogue whom we know well. His daughter, about your age," he said, looking at Rufus, "was brought back to life by Jesus. Jairus would not fabricate such a tale."

It all seemed fanciful and surreal. Who was this Jesus? Could he really raise the dead? Rufus felt his head spinning as he considered the story of the visiting Jews. In two months, he and his dad would depart for Jerusalem, and he would hopefully see for himself. Their plan would put them in the capital for Passover, and they would stay until after Pentecost. The strategy was to meet contacts that Mathias had established and made plans to buy a building for a bakery in the oldest part of the city. If everything went according to plan, Cecile and I would move later to Jerusalem, where Jesus's notoriety was quickly spreading, despite his efforts to avoid the public eye and a seemingly inevitable encounter with the Sanhedrin. "A difficult task when you are raising dead people back to life," one of the visitors said, under his breath. Uncle Mat was particularly touched by the story of the widow from Nain. In later years, I heard him repeat it often.

***

She awoke with a start. Her eyes seemed swollen shut, and she was slow to adjust to the sunlight that beamed through her curtains. Had she been crying in her sleep? Her eyelids felt like sandpaper.

Why didn't Jesse wake me? she wondered. Had her son gone out to the barn already?

"I'll put on some breakfast and then go help him bring in the eggs," she said to no one. She lay still on her bed, her feet unwilling to make the short trip to the kitchen. With a jolt, her yesterday came rushing in like a flood. The broken fence, the horses loose, her son Jesse insisting that all would be okay…then that terrible kick to his chest by the bay horse. The force had sent him falling backward. He hit his head with a mighty blow on the feeding trough, and when she got to him, his heart had stopped beating.

"Jesse's dead." The sound of her own voice shocked her. It was no dream. She gasped and then rose to her feet, still hesitating at the thought of going into the kitchen. Instead, she stood all alone in the middle of the bedroom floor and gave way to a torrent of tears.

She did not answer the knock on the door.

"Miriam, let us in," came a voice she recognized as that of her sister. "We have traveled all night to be with you." Miriam got up from her knees and lifted the latch on the door. "We left as soon as the news reached us. Show me the boy."

"In there…in the kitchen." Miriam pointed and nodded her head in the direction of the tiny kitchen. A low moan escaped from the sister. Miriam's only son lay lifeless on the table. Miriam peeked in the doorway. "My beautiful boy," she managed to whisper.

"Take courage, Miriam. We have work to do," her sister answered.

As the sun sank low in the sky, friends gathered for the burial procession. The tombs of Nain were located on the far slope of the hill that the little village perched upon. After a while of somber, silent walking, a cackle of laughter broke in on the funeral march. It was distant, but it could not be mistaken. Someone was laughing. There, coming toward them was a band of men and women making their way up the hills toward her town. They were surely oblivious to her plight. "This is no day for laughter," she muttered.

As the two groups closed the distance between them, she noticed that the leader of the group below had seen them and was raising his hand for silence. The man and His now-quiet followers stood off to the side of the trail so the funeral procession could pass by. Reverently, they lowered their heads. But the one in the lead was looking directly at her. He would not shift his gaze. As the two groups came side by side, He stepped out and took her by the arm. "Stop," was all He said.

Without a word, He led her to the side of the litter that held her dead son. To her astonishment and disgust, He reached under the shroud. Then! What was this? Everyone gasped as He drew out the dead man's handheld in His own. That was enough for Miriam. She pulled away and stomped in the dust, raising her small fist at the intruder who was…yes! He was smiling. She was just about to let her words fly when she heard a familiar voice.

"Mother!" said Jesse.

Suddenly the laughter she had noticed from afar was coming from within her as joy spilled from her lips in glad shrieks and loud peals of the most inexpressible happiness she had ever known. She gathered her son into her frail arms and cradled him like she did when he was a small child. Dizzy with excitement, she turned to the man who had stopped the funeral. He raised a finger to His lips and simply said, "Be on your way home, for this is a day for laughter!"

Thus, it was that the two groups merged into one and made their way back up the hill to Nain, led by one man—laughter their language springing up from their souls.

***

And so the fame of Jesus, the miracle worker, was quickly spreading. Despite trying His best to keep a low profile, news of the resurrection at Nain traveled far and fast. People readily put themselves in the shoes of the woman who thought she had lost everything, only to have it back again… A miracle indeed.

Trouble Brewing

Jesus and Lazarus
"Is it dead?"

The two men had been friends since childhood. They had spent countless hours together, usually with their fishing lines in the water. Lazarus loved to fish. It was one activity he could easily do. Rough games played by other boys were not possible for Lazarus. He was lame in both legs ever since birth. While many children in the neighborhood teased him, Jesus was always kind and understanding. Lazarus had something wrong with his breathing also. Often, after only a few steps, he would lean over his crutches, trying desperately to catch his breath. Jesus had fashioned the wooden crutches for His friend in His father's carpentry shop. He had also made a wooden pushcart to transport Lazarus to the village on their many excursions into town. They were quite a sight together, disappearing down the gravel road.

"Slow down," said Martha, Lazarus's older sister.

"Don't worry, Martha!" the young Jesus would call back over His shoulder.

Jesus threw a knowing wink at Lazarus, and the pair would be off for the day, nearly tripping at every turn. Their laughter could still be heard when they were well out of sight.

"I'll have supper on the table when you return," Martha would call to the wind.

One such day, Jesus and His friend happened to find a bird lying on the path in the woods.

"Is it dead?" Lazarus asked.

"It would appear so," replied Jesus, taking the bird into His hands.

Jesus cradled the pitiful creature and then seemed to whisper something as He held it up to the blue sky above. After a moment, the little creature spread its wings and flew away.

"I guess it wasn't dead after all," said Lazarus.

Jesus smiled and looked straight into his eyes. "Perhaps not, but there are things that are stronger than death."

Jesus drew close to his friend. They both knew this was a conversation to remember.

"Death is not the end," Jesus spoke with authority. "Dead things come alive!"

Watching the bird fly out of sight, Jesus again turned to face His astonished friend.

"You will need to remember that one day." There was a seriousness to the sound of Jesus's voice.

Their friendship grew as the years went by. Boyhood games were traded for adult discussions around the dinner table, especially after Lazarus's family moved to Nazareth for a number of years. They later moved again, this time to Bethany. Jesus was a frequent guest in their home, especially on the nights when Martha was cooking. Lame

Lazarus would sit for hours talking with his friend. His younger sister Mary would join the group at the table, always quiet and listening. Martha would bustle about, always on her feet...always serving. As time went by, the discussions deepened to cover some amazing occurrences involving Jesus. It seems He was claiming now to be the Son of God and He was working miracles to back up the claim. Lazarus would study his friend's face on evenings like this, looking intently—trying to measure the sincerity of Jesus. He wanted to believe, but it seemed impossible. Jesus had no friends in the power structure, and His only companions were a rough-and-tumble group of fishermen and farmers. Occasionally, one or two of these disciples would come to the house with Jesus. These were intense times, and Lazarus lamented that his condition kept him increasingly house-bound. He was worsening with time, that much was obvious, yet he still leaned in and listened carefully to the dinner talks until...

"Off to bed for you, Lazarus." It would always be Martha sending him off to his bedroom in the back of the house.

"Oh, sister, it's early yet," he would protest.

"You need to get stronger, and sleep will help with that!" she would counter.

He knew arguing was pointless. Martha ran a tight ship.

"I will be back to visit soon," Jesus would say to His tired friend. "Sleep well."

"Why won't you heal him?" Mary asked Jesus one night after her brother had retired to his room. "I know you can do this thing. He is getting sicker by the day. Can't you help him?"

"Oh, Mary," breathed Jesus. "Sometimes our questions have no answers until the Father in heaven reveals them."

"Will he never be well then?" Mary's question hung in the air.

Finally, Jesus spoke. "Lazarus will be more than just well. There will be a day when he will be made more alive than he has ever been."

Mary sighed and stated, "I believe in the resurrection of the dead on that final day. But I hate to see him suffer so."

"The darker the night, the brighter dawn's light," replied Jesus.

Everyone around the table nodded in agreement.

One morning, Lazarus was too weak to leave his room.

"His fever is high," fussed Martha. "I'm going to call the doctor. I am worried about our brother."

Mary brought a cool, damp cloth and laid it on Lazarus's brow.

"I will send for Jesus," she said, not taking her eyes off her brother.

A deep cough rattled in the sick man's chest. He gasped for air. He was laboring for each breath.

"I don't think that Jesus is nearby," replied Martha. "He was traveling north last we knew."

A messenger was dispatched nonetheless. Hope against hope, the sisters watched at the bedside of Lazarus. Each breath came more slowly than the last. And then there were none.

***

They laid him in a tomb and mourned for him. Jesus and his followers arrived several days later—seemingly too late to intervene until…

"Lazarus, my friend. Come out here!"

The voice calling for him was familiar, but it seemed oddly distant. Jesus, whose voice he now recognized, had called his name a hundred times from the portico outside his home near Nazareth.

"I must have been more tired than I thought," considered Lazarus. "Did I really dream of angels?"

He heard the voice of Jesus calling again. But where was He? He tried to call back to his friend, but there was something covering his mouth. Peeling it away, he managed a response. "Coming, Jesus!"

Where were his crutches? Why could he not see? This was not his room in the back of their house.

"Here, let me help you with those wrappings." The voice belonged to a man dressed in white.

He had a glowing inner light that radiated around the place where Lazarus lay.

"This is a tomb!" Lazarus whispered the words.

"Yes, it is," said the one helping him unwind the cloth strips that were wrapped around him.

"Am I dead, then?" asked Lazarus.

"You were," replied the glowing man. "But our Lord has called you back to earth life. Now go forth."

"Are you an angel?" Lazarus asked the question as he was led to the mouth of the burial cave.

The man just smiled and said, "You won't recall where you have been, but you will see it again in time."

"I remember it was beautiful." Lazarus was trying to clear his thoughts.

"That it is," said the man. "I am returning there now."

As Lazarus stepped out of the tomb, he realized he had left his crutches behind. He had no need of them. He took a deep gulp of fresh air and fell into the embrace of his friend. Jesus and Lazarus were beyond happy. The two began walking arm in arm the mile or so to the house, leaving the astonished sisters and the disciples to stand and wonder. Their laughter could still be heard when they were well out of sight.

***

"Death is swallowed up by life!" he was known to say.

It is said that in his elder years, old Lazarus was brought up on charges by those seeking to snuff out the early church. Threatened with execution if he continued proclaiming the new gospel, Lazarus laughed. He could be heard laughing still as he walked out of sight.

"Dead things come alive," they heard him say as his words floated back on the wind.

Thus, the raising of Lazarus was spoken of in Jerusalem and as far away as Cyrene.

In Bethany, to the northeast of Jerusalem, Lazarus was the talk of the town. He was alive—there could be no doubt about that. The question on everyone's mind was, Had he truly been dead? According to his claim and that of his family, he had died. The fact that he was walking about and being very visible around the town was attributed to a miracle. It was Jesus who had gone to the grave where Lazarus had lain lifeless for nearly a week and called him forth from the tomb. What happened next was the source of the uproar. Lazarus walked out into the light of the day.

"It's a trick!" called one voice in the crowd that had followed Jesus to the grave.

"Beautifully staged, but nothing more than a hoax," hollered another.

"Why not raise the whole cemetery if you are for real," came another scoffer's voice.

The men who contested the resurrection had come from the temple in Jerusalem. They were religious leaders, normally reserved and stately. Now they were loud and unruly. They were at odds with the Nazarene, Jesus. He had been publicly denouncing them to the Jewish populace, and they were fed up, both with him and his followers.

Still they could not explain the nagging question in their heart, "What if it was all true?" The questions only grew deeper as the story of Lazarus began to spread far and wide.

***

The pharisaical community was rapidly losing their privileged position in the religious order of Jewish life. Most of them were old and worn. A popular phrase heard from worshippers went something like, "We think some of the religious leaders began serving while Solomon was emperor." The Sadducees were a more youthful lot, and their energy and ideas produced followers. Around the temple, it was the Sadducees who were now considered to be the reigning elite, and their belief system was sure and certain—there was no resurrection of the dead. Not now, not ever. The little widow from Nain was a manageable problem, not many had been eyewitnesses of the so-called death-to-life revival of her son. Jesus of Nazareth was credited with that miracle, but he was keeping a low profile. Lazarus was a bigger concern. He was visible and loud. And very much alive.

"One more resurrection and we will be in real trouble with the masses," said a letter from a cleric outside the region, addressed to the temple priests in Jerusalem. "We will have to make sure that doesn't occur. We can ill afford the predictable results," came the reply.

This resurrection event, staged or not, was the last straw for the leadership at the temple in Jerusalem. They sent for Lazarus and questioned him for hours, trying to break him down. They sent a temple guard of twelve men to try and bring in Jesus Himself but He and His men had disappeared over the border into Syria.

"Nothing but a well-presented magic trick," they stated in their public gatherings.

Still, many in Israel believed a miracle had transpired and that Jesus was their soon and coming king.

"We do not need a king," said the Sadducees in reply. "We have no king but Caesar."

At one improvised gathering outside the temple, a man named Jesus Barabbas was arrested for inciting the crowd by denouncing Rome.

"Can Caesar raise a dead man?" he called to fellow Jews in the crowded courtyard.

Soon others joined him, and a riot began to break out. According to one eyewitness, Barabbas grabbed a rock and hurled it at the Roman officer who was trying to subdue the protesters. The missile hit the soldier in the jaw and knocked him from his horse. Injured, but alive, the man was carried to safety, and Barabbas was placed under arrest.

The Sadducees went straight to Pilate, the Roman governor, and attempted to convince him that Barabbas was a supporter of Jesus of Nazareth.

"He has secret supporters everywhere," the priests confided, "some within our own circle."

"That's your problem—not mine," the governor shot back.

Nonetheless, a curious Pilate ordered Barabbas be brought to him for private questioning.

"Jesus who?" spat the prisoner when Pilate asked him the question. "I follow no man. I just hate Romans."

He was subsequently locked up again, this time, awaiting trial. Pilate was plenty worried about the unrest in the streets, and he was glad to be able to report back to Rome that he had at least one ringleader locked away in the dungeon. As for the fallen centurion that was struck by the rock, he was treated for a broken jaw and some missing teeth, but the local physician said he would make a full recovery. The army of Rome stationed soldiers throughout the city, a visible reminder that no one would be spared punishment if they dared cross the line of acceptable behavior.

Pilate was also becoming more and more curious about the Nazarene, Jesus. He had not met the man, but he intended to do so. For the life of him, he could not understand the Sanhedrin's hatred for this Jesus.

"Just a misguided carpenter, isn't he?"

Pilate was speaking to Caiaphas, the High Priest, the rabbi who held the senior position in the religious hierarchy of the Jewish religion. The two met once a month to keep communication flowing between the temple and the governor's palace.

"What is he guilty of?" asked Pilate.

Caiaphas hissed back, "He claims he has raised the dead."

"Hardly a crime, unless it is my predecessor he causes to return from hell," Pilate said as he looked about the room to see who was enjoying his attempt at humor.

Some of the guards smiled and chuckled uncomfortably. It was unwise to take sides in personal matters in the governor's mansion. Intrigue and drama were part of the job, and one had to be careful. Pilate's disdain for the last governor of Israel was widely known. The two men had been political rivals and had sharp disagreements on more than one occasion. The older of the two, Valerius Gratus, had been promoted to governor of the Jewish state ahead of Pilate. However, he did not govern long. He died of a fever from an infected wound after little more than one year in Judea. Caesar promptly sent Pilate to fill the vacancy, a move Pilate interpreted as a recognition of his superior talents. However, current reports on Caesar's desk from the city of Jerusalem warned of civil disobedience and a public discord. Pilate was expected to keep the lid on things, but the pot was definitely starting to boil over. With the observance of Passover just around the corner, Pilate knew he would have a host of pilgrims and worshippers from all over the world descending on Jerusalem. He realized he could ill afford an uprising during the holy days. If one got started, no one could tell where it would end. The Romans well remembered the Jewish revolt in Cyrene, and Caesar wanted no similar situation to befall his regime as had occurred years ago.

These current Jews of Jerusalem were passionate but, to this point, unorganized. They needed only a leader to rally them together. Pilate shuddered as he considered the potential for disaster.

"We can't let them get a united effort underway," he said aloud in his room. "I've got to take the Nazarene out of the picture."

Summoning his commander, he turned and said, "Find me this Jesus of Nazareth."

SETTING SAIL

Mathias, Simon, and Rufus
"The docks were already busy."

"They said that Jesus was over the Syrian border to the north. He's keeping a low profile, for certain." It was Mathias who shared the news to a small group of men in Simon's bakeshop.

"Who spoke that to you?" asked Simon as he pulled some fresh loaves out of the brick oven at the Top Shelf.

"The travelers who came here to Cyrene recruiting zealots in order to return with them to Jerusalem." Mathias was reflecting on the visit by the men from Bethany.

The discussion ever since their departure was focused on the reports of unrest in Jerusalem.

"We picked a dandy time to test the market in Israel," Simon whined. "We will probably be thrown in jail ourselves."

"For what?" His brother-in-law laughed. "Charging too much for a cupcake?"

Simon had to crack a smile but said plainly, "I plan to steer clear of any rabble-rousing, Mathias." Simon was very serious now. "Especially since I will be bringing Rufus with us. I hope it was a good decision to bring the boy."

"He's now a man, Simon," said Mathias.

Looking at Rufus clearing tables and taking orders, he added, "He will be fine. We will see to that."

The months turned into weeks and the weeks became days. Before long, it was time for the men to sail from Cyrene to Jerusalem, stopping first in Egypt, on the southern Israeli border. From there, they would go overland to their destination. It was not a long voyage, but it was the first sea venture for Rufus, and he could hardly contain his excitement. Our family left home a day before they were to set sail. There were tearful goodbyes with neighbors and friends, many of whom stood in the street waving until the carriage was out of sight. We arrived in the port city of Apollonia later that evening. It was a bustling seaside city, filled with taverns and restaurants. We selected one that looked pleasant and enjoyed a fine meal as a family, with table conversation that was born in the excitement and anxiety of coming separation. After walking down to the wharf, they located the boat that was to provide their passage to Cairo in the morning. Rufus had never seen anything more majestic. The ship was designed for transporting people, not heavy cargo. Its sleek lines were designed to cut through currents and crosswinds without sacrificing speed.

"I can't wait to sail!" remarked Rufus.

We stayed the night there in the former ghettolike seaside shantytown that had grown under Rome's economic influence to be a bustling port. The three travelers were up with the break of dawn, and together with mother and me, we walked briskly back down to the waterfront. The docks were already busy as the fishing boats unloaded their predawn catches and the fish hawkers made their sales by the barrel full. Simon led the way to a loading dock and threw their packs aboard. They boarded with a dozen other travelers, and before long, the call came from the captain to hoist anchor and set sail.

I stood on the wharf and waved to the trio as they stood along the ship's rail. As nimble as the boat had seemed at the dock, it was even more impressive on the open water. The one-masted square-sailed "gauloi" on which they sailed was a beautiful product of the Phoenician shipyards.

"First-class comfort," said Mathias as he explored the boat. "It is nothing like my heavy-duty crafts that sail the cold seas of Britannia. Those vessels are rugged, but this ship will glide us across the sea like we are floating on air."

Rufus stood at the rail as the sails unfurled, and the ship pulled away from the docks. He waved to his mother and me until we appeared as specks on the landscape. Before long, the horizon and all that was familiar was swallowed up by the wide expanse of the blue-green Mediterranean Sea.

Simon met his son up near the bow and pointed in the direction of Cyrene.

"You can no longer see home because of the arc of the earth," he said. "The world is not flat as many think it is. It is more like a ball."

Pointing to the east, he explained, "We cannot see what is ahead of us, my son. But as we get closer, it will come into view. So it will be with your life—the future will become clear as it gets closer. Be patient and things will come into focus."

"Aye," said Mathias as he joined Simon and son at the front of the vessel. "The future unfolds for each man according to the will of God."

Rufus had not heard his uncle speak of God before. He looked at him now and heard him say softly, "Jerusalem… We will see what future you hold for us."

After nearly three days at sea, the ship sailed past the Egyptian city of Alexandria and then entered the wide mouth of the famed Nile River, heading for their destination in Cairo. Rufus saw the ancient pyramids of Giza as they journeyed upriver, passing by the mysterious structures. He was in awe of their size and splendor and he asked his Uncle Mat a myriad of questions about them. The silent staring Sphinx with its eroded sides overlooked the great plain, as if it was the recorder of history, watching it unfold before its mute visage. Shepherds trudged through the gravel and sand with their flocks of bleating goats keeping pace coming down from the high country and heading for the lush vegetation on the banks of the Nile.

Simon, Rufus, and Mathias
"The silent, staring Sphinx."

Mathias, who had travelled the route many times before, told Rufus fascinating accounts of the history of Egypt. Rufus listened to tales of the beautiful Queen Cleopatra and the great pharaoh Amenhotep whose wisdom and wealth rivaled that of King Solomon himself. He spoke of Tutankhamen, the boy king who tried to remain hidden from public view.

"He was stricken with a disease that made his body deformed," said Mathias. "He was frail and died without a successor. Some believe that Moses who grew up as a prince of Egypt was adopted by King Tut's sister in hope that he would replace the ailing pharaoh. When Tut knew he was dying, it is said that he fashioned the most elaborate sarcophagus to be buried in. The face, tradition tells us, was made of solid gold. If he could not be beautiful in life, the boy king would be beautiful in the afterlife."

"Is that all true?" Rufus asked his uncle.

"Who is to say?" came the reply. "The sands of time have swept away the Golden Age of Egypt. The truth lies buried and so we tell stories that have been passed down through the years."

"There is so much to learn!" Rufus said, shaking his head.

"That is how I felt after listening to the rabbi Jesus in Jerusalem," said Uncle Mat. He had a faraway look in his eyes as he spoke. "Perhaps we will get to hear him teach again."

Reaching Cairo, they disembarked and caught on with a caravan of Greek traders who were heading for Jerusalem in order to arrive by Passover, just three weeks away.

"This should put us where we need to be with about a week to prepare," said Simon, studying the map he had purchased.

Cairo was a fascinating city, and Rufus was hesitant to depart. He explored the narrow streets and tiny shops. He tasted coffee for the first time at a store owned by a man from Burma. He saw the ruins of the ancient part of the city—the once great and flourishing territory of Memphis. Rufus pondered the well-known dramatic history that linked Egypt with Cyrene, as father recounted the historical tale.

"It was shortly after the Greeks established their presence in northern Africa as a major force for expanding Grecian culture that the Pharaoh Hophra of Egypt marshaled an army to invade Cyrene. The Greeks successfully defended their cities and beat back the Egyptians. So humiliated were the armies of Egypt that they forced Hophra from his palace and killed him in the streets of Memphis. Now, Rufus, you are standing right where that grisly history occurred."

From the tower in the center of the city, Rufus could see the great pyramids to the east. The ancient structures truly fascinated Rufus. His head was full of questions. Who built these pyramids? Who were the mighty kings that once ruled the land of Egypt? He saw too the new construction of a Roman fortress on the edge of the Nile. The formidable presence of the Roman military was everywhere. It was Rome's world certainly but not quite in Jerusalem. Not yet.

Along the Way

Jesus Christ
"Come up and walk with me for a moment."

Jesus and His band of followers crossed over the Syrian border by nightfall. Back in Israel, they were expecting trouble. Jesus was in the lead, walking in a determined fashion.

"We should make it to Bethany in three days' time," He called back to the disciples.

"That is if we don't stop to eat or sleep," murmured the men, not loud enough for Jesus to hear.

The group that followed Jesus was not happy. They had heard the crowds calling for Jesus to make a move and to oust the Romans from their land. They had the public backing to make such a power play, ever since the miracle meal on the hills of Galilee. They imagined themselves as rulers and governors under the new regime. After three years on the road, they were ready for a change. Nights in the forested foothills of lofty Mt. Hermon or rocking in the waves on the open sea of Galilee had become commonplace for these men. Scorching heat and bitter cold were both endured, it seemed with a purpose. But now, just when the time seemed right for Jesus to make His move for power and unseat the Romans, the rabbi went underground instead.

"When do we go to Jerusalem to claim the throne?" The disciple by the name of Judas Iscariot asked the question that the others were thinking.

"I have told you, my kingdom is not of this world." Jesus did not break stride as He answered.

"That doesn't make any sense at all," Judas said to the others. "We need to move now."

Their voices quieted as a farmer walked by in the opposite direction. He had a lone sheep with him.

"Likely a stray that got away from the flock," said Matthew, one of the disciples. "He probably wonders what we are up to."

There was no more conversation as they moved down the Damascus Road, tired, confused, and unsure of where Jesus was heading.

Only Judas spoke again, muttering to himself, "No sense at all. I may be a stray myself. I may break away from this flock."

"Judas!" Jesus called his name. "Come up and walk with me for a while, my friend."

"Yes, teacher," he answered. And then he whispered, "For a while."

He jogged ahead until he was alongside Jesus.

"I was getting lonely," said Jesus.

"I am with you," said Judas, hoping he was telling the truth.

***

Far to the south, near the Egyptian border, a different group of travelers was bedding down for the night. Rufus, Simon, and Uncle Matt were getting closer to the international border between Egypt and Israel and were making good time. They were crossing through the most remote region that they would encounter on their way to Jerusalem.

"History tells us that the children of Israel wandered in this wilderness region for forty years." It was Mathias who spoke. "The Red Sea is to our south, and the land of the Philistines is dead ahead. We should reach it in several days' time."

Rufus unrolled his mat and placed it between his father's and uncle's bed rolls.

"Tonight, we sleep under the stars," Mathias offered. "Once we cross the border, there will be plenty of inns to lodge us by night—but tonight, we rough it."

As they laid down for the night, under the Egyptian sky, Simon shared a story that he had heard his father Caleb tell him many years ago. It was the story of the Jewish patriarch Joseph who had been sold by his brothers into slavery and who had ended up as a ruler in Egypt almost as great as Pharaoh himself.

"It all happened here in this area," said Simon. "In fact, this road we travel is, no doubt, the same road that Joseph walked as a captive slave headed for Memphis."

Rufus was sleepy now, but he had one question for his father.

"That story is a wonderful tale, Father. Why have you never told it to me before?"

"I am not sure, my son," replied Simon wistfully. "I am not sure. Perhaps we will need to remember it someday."

Rufus lay down to rest. Sleep was slow to come for his mind was busy in awe and wonder over a man named Joseph and his mean-spirited brothers. The next morning, the caravan packed up. By the time the sun had climbed above the distant hills, the travelers were making progress on their way to the border. Rufus dug into his pack and pulled some cured beef out of the side pocket. It wasn't fancy like the sweet offerings at the Top Shelf Bakery, but it made for a fine breakfast.

Midmorning, the caravan stopped at a small outpost with a public well. The animals were watered, and the men and women in the entourage filled their skins with fresh water. The well was deep, and the water cool. As Rufus drank from his canteen in the shade of a grove of trees, he let his mind wander. He wondered if Joseph had stopped at this location, hundreds of years before while on his way to Egypt as a prisoner. Surely this ancient well had existed back then. He thought about the brothers who threatened to kill Joseph and, instead, how his brother Judah protested and talked the older brothers into selling him as a slave to a passing caravan heading for Egypt. He considered the amazing rise to power that Joseph had experienced there, earning the second-in-command ranking, just under Pharaoh himself.

"I have been thinking about your story of Joseph and the Pharaoh," said Rufus to his father who pulled up a stool into the shade. "It seems to be a story that has importance." Rufus continued, "I would like to know more about our history."

"We can accomplish that," said Simon.

"And religion," Rufus added.

"You had best talk to your Uncle Mat for that, my son. He seems more spiritual lately than I have ever known him to be. And you know that I pay little attention to such matters myself. Maybe we can both learn together."

Rufus looked at his father as he offered the idea. "Maybe so, maybe so," Simon replied.

As the caravan approached the Egyptian-Israeli border, Rufus's excitement grew. He spent a great deal of each day at the front of the massive line of camels, horses, and donkeys. The animals were more in number than the people. The beasts carried burdens of gum, ivory, resins, nuts, and various treasures from the African continent. Simon's packs were on the back of a huge mule they had purchased in Cairo. Bowls and pans made up the majority of the load. The rest they would purchase on arrival in Jerusalem.

"A sizable fortune we have in tow," said the elderly trail guide to Rufus and Mathias as they journeyed at the head of the line.

This was Rufus's favorite position. The old man had taken a liking to the young Cyrenian, and he filled his head and imagination with stories from his many years of trading and travelling. He had ventured through raids, sandstorms and shipwrecks and had the scars to prove it. Amil, who was sixty-eight years old (as best he could determine), was nimble and strong with a jagged scar that ran from his forehead to his chin.

"A Mongolian got me good when I was a young man—but I got the better of him in the end," Amil told a curious Rufus.

"Did you kill him? Did you kill the Mongol?"

Rufus was quickly hushed by Uncle Mathias who took him by the arm. "You don't query a man about such things," he whispered in the lad's ear. "Some things are private."

Rufus was a bit embarrassed, and he walked with his head down for a while.

"Come up here with me, Rufus." It was Amil who spoke. "Come and take the reins for a while… I will show you how it's done."

Needing no second invitation, Rufus climbed up the side of the aged camel who, upon Amil's command, knelt in the grass to allow Rufus aboard. It was a huge animal, bigger than any camel Rufus had seen in his homeland. It was a bit unnerving at first, but Rufus was quick to learn how to pace the caravan and keep the animals happy and moving. Soon, he was talking to the lead animal, coaxing her along. Rufus noticed that Amil had fallen asleep next to him in his seat. The snoring sounded funny to young Rufus, and he laughed aloud. His laughter caught in his throat, however, as suddenly the camels balked. A spear buried itself in the leather of his saddle horn. Rufus was looking straight into a group of eight or ten men on horseback blocking the roadway.

"This is not good," said Amil, who had quickly awakened from his dozing. He handed Rufus down to Mathias and hissed, "Get to the back of the caravan. I will handle this."

Mathias and his frightened nephew scurried to the rear.

"What is happening?" Rufus's voice was full of fear.

"Bandits," replied Mathias.

They found Simon in the rear of the troop, and the three stood still and waited.

Several minutes passed. No sound could be heard from the front of the caravan, where the robbers had blocked the road. Then, a shocking sound like thunder roared in their ears. The animals screamed, and smoke covered the entire area.

"What was that?" Simon whistled low as he asked the question.

After another silence that seemed like forever, the call came down the line. "All clear! Advance!"

Dutifully, the line began to move again. Amil came hobbling back to the rear to check on Rufus.

There he described what occurred. "They wanted gold, and they were going to try and steal whatever else they could get their hands on. I told them that I would throw down a box of money—but what I threw was a box I purchased in Greece. They call it Greek Fire, and it's hard to get your hands on. I had a friend who served in the army of Greece, and he was able to supply me with some. It's a mixture that explodes under pressure. I threw it at the bandits. Just as they were about to retrieve it, the thing went off. They disappeared as fast as could be…holding their ears and rubbing their eyes. I never actually used it before so I wasn't sure it would work. But I'll say it did!" The old man chuckled. "They won't bother us again."

As the caravan moved past the site where the would-be bandits had stopped the travelers in their tracks, the grass was still burning, as were the shrubs and bushes along the edges of the pathway.

Mathias spoke, "I have heard of this Greek Fire. Some say Alexander, son of the Macedonian Phillip, used it to strike fear into the ranks of opposing armies."

"It surely seems to have that effect," offered Simon.

Rufus was still shaking from his close call with the spear that sunk into his saddle minutes ago.

"Do you think they were trying to kill me, Father?"

Simon put his arm around the boy. "No, I think they wanted to get your attention," Simon replied. "If they wanted to kill you, believe me, they would have. Rome patrols this road fairly well. They see the thieves as being bad for business. Therefore, they keep the robbers at bay so traders like us can move through with no trouble. This group did not want to harm us. They did want to steal from us though. Stealing and murder together, however, will be punished most severely by the Romans."

Not long after the incident, the caravan passed into Israel. Just over the border, the progress became easier. The road was paved with cobblestones.

"One of Rome's better ideas," Mathias said.

About a mile from the border, they came upon the horrific remnants of a crucifixion. Several men hung on poles that were thrust into the ground. They were surely dead, and the smell of rotting flesh was in the air. Vultures had gathered and were poking and pulling at the corpses. They had been publicly executed along the roadside. A sign lay against one of the victims. It simply read, "Thus it is with thieves." It was signed by Pontius Pilate.

"The Roman governor," mused Simon.

"One of Rome's worst ideas…crucifixion," said Mathias.

Rufus stared at the dead men hanging in agonizing positions, clear testimony to the awful ends they came to.

"The Romans use this torture on those who receive the sentence of death," Uncle Mathias said in somber fashion. "It is surely a hard way to die."

"Why are they put to death on the main roadway?" Rufus asked.

"To show the power of Rome over its citizens and to serve as an example to others who may be tempted to break the law," answered Mathias.

Rufus could not help but stare at the torture and gore along the roadside. Such savagery was not shocking to the young man. He had seen his fair share at the coliseum in Cyrene. He recalled Thomas of Thera, and once again, his mind replayed the brutal end he came to at the hands of the Egyptian warrior. Rufus shuddered and walked past the dead men lining the thoroughfare.

The Bribe

Judas Iscariot
"If you can set the trap, we will arrest this Jesus of Nazareth."

While the caravan drew closer to Jerusalem, Jesus and his followers were coming to the same city but from the north. Jesus knew his enemies awaited a chance to arrest him. As focused as he was, he could not resist the cry of a blind man on the edge of the crowd. Again, it was Uncle Mathias who gathered the details of the story of that blind man outside the city of Jericho. He befriended the man years later, and now, his story must be shared within the story I tell of Rufus. Hence, you shall know it too.

***

Timaeus, or Tim as he was known in the village, was very fond of his young son. He had a deep affection for the awkward, sometimes invasive behavior that the boy had exhibited since "the dreadful mistake," as Tim called it. The mistake was his own fault. Timaeus always considered that he was the one responsible. Years ago, he had noticed some discoloration in his son's eyes and that they were irritated much of the time. Timaeus, following the advice of a relative, took his young son to a medical man in another village. The self-appointed physician decided to cure the problem with a mixture of mercury, herbs, and acid. The mixture was prepared and applied, covering the boy's eyes in a slimy paste. When the would-be doctor rinsed away the potion, Tim's little son was left sightless. He was six years old.

Timaeus spent all his free time with his blind son. Timmy Two was how he was known to the villagers. He was a loud youth. It seemed that the loss of his sense of sight caused him to overcompensate with sheer vocal volume. You could hear Timmy Two from across the marketplace, carrying clearly over the noise of the pushcart fish hawkers and the droning hum of the shoppers. The only place he was ever known to be quiet was down at the shore. There he would sit for hours, listening for the sound of his father's voice. Timaeus was the captain of a fishing vessel that ventured out on the great lake early each morning before dawn. The blind child would awaken to an empty house and begin to fix himself breakfast. His father had taught him how to fetch an egg from the chicken coop. He knew just where the wood for the stove was kept, and he dutifully stoked the fire in the hearth while he waited for his egg to boil. He was alone at these times. He never knew his mother. She had no place in his memory nor his heart. Timaeus never spoke of her.

Timmy Two spent his days in the village marketplace. He was well-known as a "nudge" to the vendors. Always underfoot, he would pass the hours waiting for the afternoon sun to feel cooler on his brow, a sure sign that evening was coming. That could mean but one thing. His father would be coming in with the day's catch. Timmy Two would head for the docks and await the familiar sound of his abba, calling orders to his crew. As soon as the ship was near enough, the silent boy would exchange listening for calling. "Abba, do you see me?" he would cry, waving his arms above his head.

The senior Tim would wave back and call, "Coming, child! Let us go home together!"

As soon as the ship docked, Timmy Two would follow the sound of his abba's calling voice and run to his open arms. His father would then take his boy's hand in his strong grip and gently lead Timmy Two through the narrow streets. An unlikely pair, they were ship captain and blind boy together on their way home.

This is how it was until the day his father's ship did not return to port. No one was sure what had happened to the captain and his crew. The blind child would not be moved from the dock where he waited silently for days on end. He sat, listening for the familiar sound of his abba, calling to him. But the sound did not come. The days became weeks, and the weeks became months. In time, the months turned to years. Timmy Two began the descent downward to the only life available to him…life on the street. He became a beggar. A blind beggar, known still as the son of Timaeus, or Bartimaeus.

His condition was dreadful. He was pitied by many but ignored by most. The mystery of his long-lost father disappeared into yesterday's news. The past was indeed a sad mystery, but the future was certainly bleaker still. His home was the streets of Jericho, where he had journeyed on the notion that people would be more generous in that city than in the small town of his birth. He remained poor, however. Occasionally coins were tossed his way, which he kept in a leather pouch until he had collected enough to buy bread from the baker.

"Alms, alms for a blind man," Bartimaeus would call.

His loud voice carried throughout the market, causing some to give way to the annoyance. "Hush, loudmouth!" they would say.

Their words had no effect. The beggar called for aid despite their rude protests. Thus, the years rolled on and on.

One morning in the marketplace, Bartimaeus heard a commotion. There were excited voices discussing a recent visit by two disciples of a rabbi named Jesus, who was said to be a miracle worker. The duo that had come to the village had spoken in glowing terms of this rabbi, claiming He was the promised Messiah. Bartimaeus did not hear of it personally as they had set up in the synagogue—a place he was not welcomed. However, in the wake of their visit, he caught some reference to Jesus giving sight to the blind. Could this be? His heart ached with curiosity.

That night, he slept fitfully. He dreamed of his father. In his dream, he was a boy again, walking home from the docks, his hand tucked snugly in his abba's strong grip. When he awoke, it was mid-morning. He could tell the hour by turning his face to the warm sun. For some reason, on this morning, the market was strangely quiet. It seemed nearly empty.

"Where is everyone?" he asked no one in particular.

Just then, a loud cheer could be heard out by the road that led around the village.

"What could it be?" Bartimaeus asked himself.

As quickly as he could, he scurried toward the sound of excited voices.

"It's Jesus!" said a woman in the crowd.

The blind beggar was close enough to hear her say. "He's coming right this way!"

Something burst inside of Bartimaeus. He began to cry out, his loud voice carrying over the crowd. "Jesus! Can you see me?"

Bartimaeus was wildly waving his arms above his head.

"Be still, beggar," said one nearby.

Another fumed, "Hush, loudmouth," and pushed him down in the dust.

But Bartimaeus could not be silenced.

His booming voice rose higher still. "Son of David! Have mercy on me. Son of David, have mercy on this blind man!"

Suddenly the crowd drew quiet. Bartimaeus strained his ears, trying to discern what was happening. Everything was still.

And then, a voice next to him said, "He's calling for you."

Then another voice, "Yes, Timmy Two. The rabbi is calling for you."

The crowd began to push him forward, parting like a wave to let him through.

"Hurry!" they urged, but Bartimaeus needed no urging.

He began to run toward a voice that he could now hear clearly.

"That's right! Come to me, son."

The sound of it reminded him of his abba's voice. He fell to the ground, embracing the rabbi's feet.

"What do you want me to do for you?" asked Jesus.

"I want to see!" sobbed the beggar.

"Do you believe I can do this for you?" asked the rabbi.

"Yes, yes," came the reply.

"Then you shall have what you ask for," said Jesus.

At that moment, Bartimaeus looked up into the gentle face of his healer… It was a smile that he could see! Looking around at the astonished crowd, he bellowed, "*I can see*!"

Cheers ascended from the people, praising this great gift. Men thumped Bartimaeus on the back. Women hugged him for joy. But Bartimaeus would not turn from the face of Jesus.

"Come with me," said the rabbi. "My Father is very fond of you."

As he slipped his hand into the strong grip of Jesus, the crowd began to move again, following an unlikely pair. They were Jesus, the son of David, and Bartimaeus, a child of God…together on their way home.

The road to Jerusalem was a rugged one indeed. Yet upon arrival outside the gates, Jesus found it to be an extremely emotional time. He halted at the crest of the Mount of Olives overlooking the city of Jerusalem. It was clear that he was crying. His followers stood awkwardly behind him and kicked at the dirt. Jesus was bent low over the burro He was riding. Suddenly, he lifted up his voice and called out, "Oh, Jerusalem, you have missed your visit from heaven. I tried to tell you, but you wouldn't listen. Now it is too late."

No one moved for what seemed an eternity. Judas Iscariot could not believe his ears. "The apple is right for the picking!" he snapped. "What are we waiting for?"

Judas then whispered something to Peter, who appeared to be dozing under the sun's heat.

"I wanted to gather you together like a mother hen and teach you the ways of the Father, but you had no ears to hear. Too late, too late." Jesus sobbed.

Something snapped inside Judas. He turned to Matthew and said, "We are so close to a coup, and our fearless leader is now backing down. 'Too late,' he says. Well, I say the time is now!"

With that, Judas retreated from the band of disciples and ran down the slope to the city. Little did he know that the Roman governor had informants planted around Jerusalem, watching for any appearance of Jesus or his followers. In the tavern that Judas entered, one such lookout recognized him. He hastily ducked out the bar and ran to the temple.

"One of his men is in the city!" he told the priest.

"Are you certain?" the priest leaned into the face of the informant as if examining a ripened fruit.

"I know the man called Judas Iscariot, and I surely saw him just now. The rest must be close by."

"Follow him and see if he leads us to Jesus."

The priest sent the man back to the older part of the city where he had spotted Judas. He was still at the tavern, where he had the ear of a dozen or so of the patrons. He was rallying the men to come together and attempt to throw the Romans out of Israel. Passover was a week away, and the Jewish population would be two or three times what it normally was. Visitors and pilgrims would crowd the streets and inns.

"A perfect time to take back what is ours."

Judas had the group of zealots at a fever pitch.

"Here! Here! We owe no allegiance to Caesar!"

The patrons of the establishment were growing louder. Judas saw that he had a following.

"What about your rabbi from Nazareth? What about Jesus the miracle worker?" someone hollered above the din.

"He is backing down," said Judas. "We cannot count on him."

"Then who will lead us?" called the crowd.

At that, the men began talking amongst themselves, and the impromptu meeting broke up. The temple spy drew closer and grabbed Judas by the arm.

"So you are not following Jesus of Nazareth any longer?" he asked Judas. "I have friends in the Sanhedrin who would pay handsomely to be able to put him behind bars for the Passover… You know, to keep his influence off the streets."

"An easy task," replied Judas.

"Maybe, if we could find him," said the informant.

"How much money are we talking about?" asked Judas.

"Come with me to the temple and let them tell you themselves," the man urged Judas.

With that, the pair headed out into the street and moved from the old city to the temple area.

At the temple, Caiaphas the chief priest was very interested in what Judas had to say. Annas, the father-in-law of Caiaphas and former high priest, was summoned to also hear the matter. The Romans did not trust Annas and had pressured the Sanhedrin to remove him from power some ten years earlier. He had not gone far, however, and to many Jews, he was still the go-to person in temple affairs. The two men listened as Judas spoke of the crowds calling for Jesus to be king and his hesitancy to embrace the power.

"We, too, want to throw off the Roman yoke," said Annas dryly. "But these matters require patience and wisdom. One doesn't walk up to Caesar and say, 'Remove yourself.'"

Then, Caiaphas leaned toward Judas and said, "If you can set the trap, we will arrest this Jesus of Nazareth and hold him behind bars until the Passover festival is over. That way, he will not upset any apple carts by acting prematurely. His intentions are no doubt good, but you can see he has no relationship to the power structure and is doomed to fail. You will be doing your country a big favor if you trust us to handle Rome and this Jesus."

"What will be the charge when you arrest him?" Judas asked.

"Leave that to us," replied Caiaphas in a way that made Judas shudder.

The high priest then handed Judas a bag and winked.

"A hefty sum for your cooperation," Annas said to Judas as Caiaphas dismissed him with a handshake.

After he was out of earshot, Caiaphas turned to his father-in-law. "On the souls of my children, your grandchildren, I will get rid of this thorn in Israel's side. Better for one man to die than to destroy an entire nation."

"No one said anything about death," Annas chided.

"There was much I did not say," Caiaphas said with a long look out the window to the people flooding the temple courtyard. "We must proceed with caution. These people could turn on us if we are not careful. Jesus has rapport with the masses."

Caiaphas drifted into thought and spoke no more. It was Annas who finally broke the silence.

"No one has to die," was all he said before leaving Caiaphas alone with his thoughts.

Open for Business

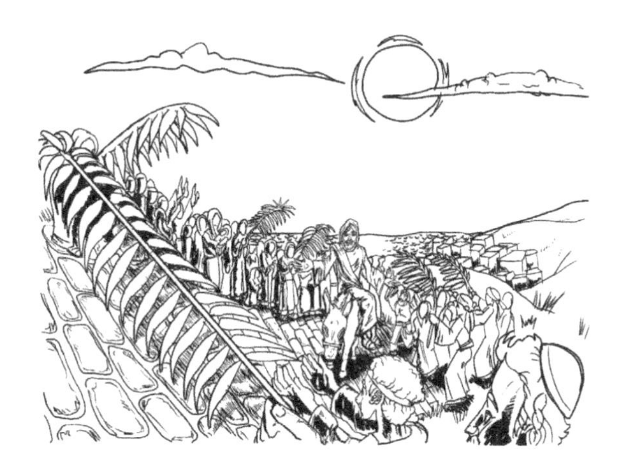

Jesus and the crowd
"Prepare the way!"

Mathias whistled low as he walked around the empty storefront in the center of the old city. The caravan of travelers had reached Jerusalem at dusk the night before. Simon, Rufus, and Uncle Mathias had found a room at an inn that was comfortable and clean.

"Lucky we are indeed," said Simon. "By week's end, there won't be a room to rent anywhere."

On the same street as the inn was the empty store where the trio now stood. Owned by the same man that owned the inn, it had recently served as a storage unit for another local businessman. Before that, it had belonged to a shipping magnate.

"Joseph from Arimathea was the original owner," said the innkeeper. "He had it as office space for his trading business. There is a large, empty room upstairs."

"I have been in this place before when Joseph and I had dealings."

Mathias was already picturing the empty space as a bakery and eatery.

"I must say, it seems perfect," Simon agreed. "But can we afford it?"

"Let me worry about that," cautioned Mathias.

The empty unit had a small room toward the back that would serve well as a kitchen. Mathias's ever-present companion, Cico, chattered excitedly on the large windowsill that overlooked the courtyard outside.

"That's the governor's mansion behind us," said Mathias.

"This part has fine ventilation," Simon said. "I could easily see this room as the kitchen. We can put the oven just outside on the courtyard, prepare food in the kitchen, and serve the public out front."

A small separate room was just big enough to serve as a storage closet.

"Rufus can hide in here when he feels lazy!" Mathias joked.

Upstairs there was a large empty room, perfect for a dining area. Simon was getting excited about the prospects for introducing Top Shelf to Jerusalem.

Rufus was smiling ear to ear. "When do we start baking?" he asked.

The two older men chuckled at the energy of the younger Rufus.

"Ah, youth!" exclaimed Mathias. "I remember it well. Let's go first and tell the innkeeper we want to rent this soon-to-be bakery."

With that, Simon headed out into the busy street, Uncle Mat and Rufus in tow.

Later that day, the threesome, along with a few hired hands, washed and painted the rented space. By midmorning the next day, the smell of baked bread wafted out the open windows to the busy street. Mathias and Rufus purchased tables and chairs from a local carpenter who had an upscale showroom and produced fine work at a good price. They arranged them nicely in the eating area and placed a few outside on the wide sidewalk.

"Just like home in Cyrene," Rufus observed.

As a finishing touch, a local artist painted "Top Shelf Bakery" over the main entrance.

"I think we are ready," said Simon, wiping the sweat from his brow. "Tomorrow, you two will hand out samples in the street and offer big discounts to everyone. We open at noon! I shall be baking all night!"

The next morning, Rufus and his uncle filled big sacks with specialty cookies from Simon's oven that had been a favorite back in Cyrene. They were sweet to the taste, made of flour, sesame oil, and honey. Flat and crispy with a soft center, they were completely kosher and certainly delicious. "I'll pass out samples down in the center of town. You hit the Eastern Gate and catch the people on their way into the city." Mathias seemed genuinely excited as he spoke to young Rufus. The pair split up, promising to meet at the temple in two hours.

Out by the gate, the crowd was larger than Rufus had expected. No one was coming in or out of the city, they just stood in a large number, as if they were waiting for something…or someone. There was a sense of anticipation in the air. The baked goods began to go quickly as Rufus offered them to folks who had been standing at the entrance for more than an hour.

I need to make an announcement to let them know where these treats come from, he thought.

He was just about to raise his voice to announce the grand opening when the crowd erupted in a cheer. "Hosanna!" The sound was deafening.

"Here they come!"

"Prepare the way!"

"Bless the Son of David!"

"Who is coming?" asked Rufus at the top of his lungs.

"It's Jesus the Nazarene!" said a woman next to him. "He comes to take the throne!"

Rufus could hardly believe his ears. Could it be that the miracle worker was coming now to enter the capital city and set up his kingship? He pushed his way through the throng and stood on the edge of the roadside, just inside the huge gate. He could see an entourage of people about to enter through the ancient passageway. They were loudly singing a Jewish folk song that Rufus did not recognize, dancing around a central figure—a man seated on a donkey. Everyone, it seemed, was taking their cloaks off and spreading them along the well-traveled road. Some climbed the palms that lined the thoroughfare and tossed down branches to many in the crowd who waved them over their heads like banners.

Just then, the man on the donkey, along with his followers, came through the gate. Rufus knew beyond a doubt that this was Jesus. The crowd pressed in to get closer, and in the melee, Rufus dropped his satchel full of baked goods. He bent down to retrieve the bag and nearly collided with some of the men in the procession. Knocked off his feet, Rufus fell to the ground and lay in the dust. A hand was offered to him, and he was pulled to his feet by a kind-faced man who was now holding the satchel.

"What have we here?"

The man brushed off the dirt from the face of young Rufus and handed him the bag. It was empty. The bakery items had spilled in the fall and were now being trampled underfoot by the raucous crowd. Rufus felt like a failure. He fought back the tears and brushed himself off. The procession was larger and louder now as Jesus entered the city. Rufus did not know what to do, but his curiosity carried him along like a ship on the sea, and he followed Jesus and the multitude to the temple.

"Hosanna!"

"Son of David!"

The cheering throng was growing in number and enthusiasm. Rufus noticed some Roman soldiers, several companies or maybe more, assuming key positions in the temple courtyard. They were preparing to act, if the mass of worshippers got too close to the palace.

Jesus, still astride the donkey, seemed lost in thought.

He had a worried look in his eyes, thought Rufus. A hand grabbed him by the shoulder, and he turned around to find Mathias standing behind him.

"Isn't this fantastic?" he asked Rufus. "This is good for business. All these people will be hungry soon, and we are ready to open just a block away from here."

Noticing the empty bag on Rufus's shoulder, he inquired as to his success in passing out the baked cookies. Rufus told his uncle of the pandemonium at the gate and how he had been knocked over, losing most of his free samples.

"Never mind that," said Uncle Mat. "I have passed out enough to feed the whole Roman army."

A commotion suddenly arose over by the Gentile courts outside the temple. Cheers turned to screams as men and women ran in all directions. Jesus, no longer riding in the procession, was storming through the temple courts, a bull whip in hand and sheer anger on His face. He overturned tables full of caged birds, opening the cages and setting the birds flapping toward freedom. He knocked over chairs, sending people scurrying for cover. Jesus flipped the money changer's tables over, and with His whip cracking over the heads of the animals waiting to be sold for sacrifice, He pulled down the banners and signs that hung in the sacred place. He was a one-man whirlwind, and everyone stood their distance. Jesus finally faced the hushed crowd.

"My Father's house is to be a place of prayer…not a den of thieves." He was breathing heavily, and His voice was tight with emotion as He spoke. No one moved for what seemed like an eternity.

Then a lame man who sat every day by the temple entrance broke the silence. "Jesus, will you heal me?" His voice echoed off the temple columns.

"Come closer to me," said Jesus who stretched out his hand and took the poor man into his arms, where he held him in an embrace.

When Jesus let him go, he stood on two strong legs and feet leaping and dancing. He shouted, "I am well! Praise the God of Israel, I am healed!"

Rufus was in awe. He and Mathias watched in silence as the blind and lame stood in line to be touched by Jesus of Nazareth.

"He is really something, isn't he?"

The voice belonged to a man standing behind Mathias and Rufus.

Turning around, Mathias smiled and grabbed the man in an embrace. "Joseph, my old friend!" exclaimed Mathias.

Turning to Rufus, Uncle Mat introduced his friend to his curious young nephew.

"This is Joseph from Arimathea," he proclaimed. "A dear friend and business partner whom I have not seen in... Has it been ten years, Joseph?"

"Maybe more," said Joseph. "I heard from the innkeeper nearby that you were in Jerusalem, but I did not expect to find you in this crowd. Praise be to God, I spotted you."

"Do we look like tourists then?" asked Mathias.

"A bit!" Joseph laughed. Then he grew serious. "Mathias, I need you to help me," said Joseph.

"Anything!" said Mathias.

"Jesus, whom you see, is my nephew. I feel obliged to protect him from some enemies in high places. Even now, the Sanhedrin are trying to convince Pilate to arrest Jesus for disorderly conduct. Pilate maintains that what just occurred here is a Jewish matter and therefore the concern of the temple. I just left a meeting with the Romans and my fellow Pharisees and they are intent on getting rid of Jesus. They call him a rabble rouser and a blasphemer. I am keeping silent, but already some of my fellow rulers are suspicious of my loyalties. The high priest Caiaphas is returning to Pilate now to hear his ruling. The governor seems to be softening. He wants nothing to go wrong during Passover. He may arrest Jesus for reasons that Rome would support. I and one other are the only two in the temple who believe Jesus of Nazareth is from heaven."

"I am coming to that belief as well," whispered Mathias, with a nod toward the blind, lame, and deaf who were being healed

A hushed awe had overtaken the once exuberant crowd.

Mathias asked, "What can we do to help you, Joseph?"

"I need to get him away from the public and hide him until evening.

"I know just the place," Rufus interjected. "Uncle Mat, the room upstairs in the bakeshop! It is perfect."

Roman soldiers began to appear in greater numbers around the edges of the crowd.

"We've got to act now," Joseph said. "We need a distraction so we can get Jesus away."

"Leave that to me!" said Mathias. "Rufus, go with Joseph. He knows the building where your father is. I will meet you there."

With that, Mathias started hollering. Pointing away from where Jesus was standing, he shouted, "*Thief!* That man stole my money!" He started pushing the crowd, crying, "Stop him!"

Seeing the opportunity and distraction, Joseph spoke in a whisper to the men around Jesus.

"Trust me, we have no time to waste," he said to Jesus who looked at him and then at Rufus. He smiled and said, "Let's go then."

All the while, Mathias was creating a commotion, pointing at no one but convincing the soldiers that he had been robbed. Joseph, Rufus, and Jesus went through the crowd unseen and, within minutes, entered the bakeshop that was due to open in an hour. Simon was shocked as the men entered his empty shop. Rufus quickly explained the plan to hide Jesus from the public eye until nightfall. Mathias came bursting through the door at that moment and said, "How was that for a distraction, Joseph?"

Then looking at Jesus, he bowed low and said, "At your service, my Lord."

Within minutes, Simon had made a comfortable space in the upstairs room. The bakery opened as scheduled at noon, with a crowd of curious patrons who sampled the items that Simon put out on trays. They soon were involved in political discussion, and for much of the afternoon, they wondered where Jesus and his followers had gone. Many had expected a march on Pilate's palace after the reception Jesus had received upon entering the gates of the city. Never would they have guessed that Jesus was within earshot of their discussions, cleverly concealed, one floor above them.

At supper hour, they closed up the shop and locked the door. They then huddled together with a lone candle burning in the kitchen, and there they ate dinner, Joseph, Jesus, Mathias, Simon, and Rufus. Simon talked of Cyrene and their journey through Egypt. Jesus told them that he had lived in Egypt as a boy, but that he did not recall much of that time for he had been very young. He remembered the grand pyramids of Giza, however, and Rufus lit up at the mention of those great edifices. Mathias told how he had been present at the miracle feeding of the masses on the Galilean hills and how he had been part of the throng that had followed Jesus as he taught the crowds about the kingdom of God. "I was being baptized by John the wilderness prophet on the day he baptized you in the Jordan," Mathias stated. "I heard thunder from heaven when you came up from the water."

"It was no accident that you were there for these events," Jesus spoke evenly. "You will someday testify to these things as if your life depended on it. And indeed it may."

Mathias nodded, and the room grew quiet for a moment.

"Can you tell us how you did that with the loaves and fish?" Rufus turned red with embarrassment as he asked the question.

"Well," replied Jesus, "did you see the sick made well by the temple this morning?"

"Yes!" all four men answered as one.

"If you have faith to accept it, then you will know I am the son of man and the son of God. I am one with my Father, and I have come to share the good news of his love with all who have ears to hear and hearts to believe."

"That kind of talk will get you in a lot of trouble at the temple, but you know that I believe you," said Joseph of Arimathea.

"As do I," added Mathias.

"And I," echoed Rufus.

Simon remained silent, but all could tell he was deep in thought. The rest of the meal was eaten in silence. It had been a long day, and fatigue was creeping in.

"I must go to Bethany now," Jesus said, standing to His feet.

Looking at Rufus, He put His strong hands on his shoulders and peered into his eyes.

"Rufus, you are young, but I have chosen you to be a leader in my church. You will not understand all that this means for a time, but it will become clear in the time to come."

Rufus felt a rush of emotion, and he began to cry.

"Save your tears for a time that is coming soon," said the Nazarene.

With that, He bade them goodbye and slipped out into the dark street headed for Bethany.

"Wait!" called Rufus. "Take some bread and cakes with you." He ran into the dark street and handed Jesus of Nazareth a small sack, featuring a variety of the bakeshop's best offerings.

"In case you get hungry along the way," he gushed as he caught up with Jesus.

"Thank you, Rufus," said the miracle worker. "I will see you again."

Back at the shop, Simon was looking over the day's receipts. "Our first day of doing business in Jerusalem was a great success!" he exclaimed.

"But we will always remember it for another reason," said Mathias.

"And he is on his way to Bethany right now, and perhaps, soon, to David's throne," added Joseph.

Rufus, coming back through the doorway, stood and stared out into the now empty street, the tears still coursing down his face.

"I will always remember this day," he said softly.

THE ROOM UPSTAIRS

Cico and Mathias
"That kind of talk will get you in a lot of trouble... but you know that I believe you," said Joseph of Arimathea.
"As do I," added Mathias.

"You had him right under your noses, and you didn't arrest him!" Judas Iscariot was angry. He leaned across the table where members of the Jewish Sanhedrin were sitting. "Jesus knocked the temple apart, and you couldn't manage a misdemeanor charge to hold him on for a few days until after the festival?"

"We waited until Pilate gave the soldiers the go ahead, but by then, he was gone. We don't know where he went," replied Caiaphas defensively.

"Bethany," fumed Judas. "Jesus is in Bethany with his followers. They are at the home of Lazarus. You should know this. Half of the nation of Israel is there hoping for another miracle or a glimpse of the once very dead, now living and breathing, Lazarus."

"If we try to arrest him when he is surrounded by an adoring crowd, we will achieve exactly the opposite of what we hope for." Caiaphas was standing and pacing the floor while he spoke. "We have to take him when he is alone. We must not allow the public to interfere. We need Pilate to authorize a battalion of soldiers to arrest him so the people will believe this is Caesar's doing and not our own. I shall convince the governor to dispatch the troops. Judas, you just tell us where we can find him alone."

"He often secludes himself when he prays," offered Judas. "And he likes to pray at the olive grove…in Gethsemane"

With that, Judas turned and left the religious leaders to plot amongst themselves. Passover was just three days away now, and the pressure was mounting on the Sanhedrin to make their move. They wanted to prove their religious authority to the followers of Jesus. They could not tolerate any more claims of deity by the Nazarene, nor could they allow Lazarus an opportunity to speak publicly.

***

The following morning, just after sunrise, Rufus awoke and looked out the window of the inn and onto the temple courtyard.

"It's Jesus!" he exclaimed.

He hastened to get dressed, being careful not to awaken his snoring uncle, and soon he padded down the stairs and out the door. In just a moment's time, he joined the small but growing crowd surrounding Jesus. He pushed his way closer and began to listen as the rabbi taught. He recalled Uncle Mat's words about how Jesus had spoken like an angel. Now he was able to hear for himself. Jesus, indeed, talked tenderly to the street people who pressed in closer as His words permeated their hearts. He uttered mysteries, but Rufus hung on every word. Someone asked a question about the violent episode the day before when Jesus had driven the cash managers out of the temple.

"My Father's house is a place for prayer, not exploitation," Jesus replied. "Besides that, you will know the Father sent me when you see me destroy this temple and rebuild it in three days."

A ripple of laughter passed through the gathering.

"Do you believe this will occur?"

Jesus was speaking more loudly now as He noticed a few elders and priests leaning over the porch railing of the temple. They were obviously not happy with the teaching. They were whispering among themselves and gesturing in animated fashion.

Looking directly at the Pharisees, Jesus began to speak with growing passion. "You see those teachers of the law?" He offered, pointing to the men at the railing. "Do what they say to do, but don't follow their example. They do not practice what they preach. They are not true sons of Abraham!"

One of the priests cupped his hands and hollered down into the courtyard. "We are certainly the sons of Abraham—and at least we know who our fathers are. We are not illegitimate, but you are!"

Jesus shrugged and turned his attention back on the crowd around him. It was then that he noticed Rufus.

"Rufus, my young friend, come closer." Jesus beckoned with his outstretched arm. The crowd parted as Rufus pushed forward toward Jesus. He stood before the teacher and smiled as Jesus put his strong arm around his shoulders.

"See this young man?" Jesus spoke to the crowd. "He has simple faith. He believes my words. He is an obedient son to his father, who by the way is a fine baker. Rufus, could you ask your father to provide me with the bread I will need tomorrow evening for the Passover meal? I would be most grateful."

Rufus could not speak. Instead, he nodded vigorously, and the crowd laughed again. Some Roman guards moved into place, joining the temple priests up along the portico. Sensing it was a good time to leave, Jesus spoke to Rufus.

"Here, I will go with you to ask this favor of Simon of Cyrene," he said, taking young Rufus by the arm and guiding him down the street to the Top Shelf Bakery.

Simon had been baking since before dawn and had a variety of confections on display in the store windows. The crowd followed Rufus and Jesus to the bakery, and before midmorning, Simon had sold his last pastry. He then readily agreed to the request to make unleavened bread for the Passover meal as Jesus had entreated.

"Good. I will send two of my disciples in the afternoon to pick up the supplies," replied Jesus.

Calling to two men who were seated nearby, he introduced them all by saying, "These two will come by tomorrow for the food. This is John and another Simon, whom we call Peter."

The men shook hands warmly as Jesus looked on. Simon could not help but notice the callouses and weather-beaten skin on the hands of the two disciples.

"I have a baker's handshake," the Cyrenian considered.

Almost as if he knew what Simon was thinking, Jesus spoke up and said, "Simon, your hands will soon feel a strain and burning that you cannot imagine. But the sacrifice you make will be remembered for ages to come."

Simon of Cyrene stammered a thank you, although he was unsure of the meaning of the words. He retreated alone to the kitchen and to his thoughts.

Just then, Mathias and Joseph of Arimathea entered the bakeshop. Approaching Jesus, they cautioned him that a group of religious leaders were gathering together and were headed toward the bakery. They planned to trap Jesus and perhaps arrest him.

"Time to go," said Jesus to his disciples as he stood to his feet.

"It is not yet my time," he said to Mathias and Joseph, "but it is coming soon. Thank you for your intervention."

Quickly the men spilled out into the early afternoon sun as they headed once more for Bethany.

The following day, the already crowded streets of Jerusalem were even more packed with pilgrims and tourists. Simon and Rufus were busy baking at the Top Shelf while Mathias stayed in the temple courtyard to see if Jesus would make an appearance. The Sanhedrin held an emergency meeting to discuss the "Jesus problem," expressing their concern that he was now more popular than they were. These were men who were accustomed to privilege and honor and were subsequently able to exert their authority over the Jewish nation, often to their own, personal profit. With the crowds turning their attention on to Jesus, the religious establishment grew more and more jealous of his popularity.

"The pharisees love the attention, not the people," Jesus had been known to say. "They steal from poor unsuspecting widows and then try to appear pious by making long prayers in public places."

Statements like that ate at the priests and elders. They met regularly to scheme a method to get Jesus out of their way. Several of the priests and elders were silent in these clandestine meetings. Joseph of Arimathea and his ally, Elder Nicodemus were both now secret, but certain believers in the claims of the Nazarene. They said not a word, but they shared glances that displayed their uneasiness with the direction the council was taking.

Mathias could feel the tension in his back growing although he was not certain as to why he felt such anxiety. A shiver ran through his body, and his head was aching. He closed his eyes as the sun rose over the temple. There was an anticipation in the streets. That was undeniable. Many Jews were gathering to see if there would be any more healings or displays of violence in the temple courtyard. While his eyes were still closed, Mathias felt a hand on his shoulder. It was Joseph.

"I fear the direction that our council seems to be moving in," said Joseph quietly.

"What began as an effort to keep the peace is now a murder plot."

"I cannot say much, but it has become obvious that many of my brothers, fueled by jealousy and hate, will be satisfied with nothing less than the death of Jesus. I have known for some time that it could get ugly, but I never suspected it would come to this."

Mathias opened his eyes and looked earnestly at his old friend. "I know that Jesus is a relative of yours, but tell me, Joseph, are you truly convinced that he is from God?" Mathias knew that this was one of the most important conversations he would ever have.

"Walk with me, Mathias," said Joseph. "Walk and I will tell you something I have rarely spoken of."

The two men left the courtyard and headed out toward the old part of the city. Joseph began.

"You know that my wife is a convert to Judaism. She is from the coastal cities to our north. We met in Tyre when I was a young sea merchant, just embarking on my career. I fell in love with her, and she with me. We married young and had two daughters, one that died from the fever when she was but an infant. The other, my Miriam, was born with a hideous disease that bound her in paralysis and seizures. It became too much for my wife to care for her, so when Miriam was just ten years of age, she and her mother left Jerusalem and went home to her family in Tyre. I was out at sea most of the time so I could offer little support. However, my niece, Mary, who, as you know, is the mother of Jesus, sent word to my in-laws that Jesus was in Tyre. This all occurred a few years ago, but it makes me weep when I speak of it even now."

Joseph sighed and then continued.

"My lovely wife went through the streets, looking for the healer, Jesus. She found Him down by the docks and she begged Him to come and see Miriam. She was persistent for Jesus was keeping a low profile in Gentile country. All I can tell you is when I next got home from the sea, my little girl was completely well. She is to this day."

Mathias gave a low whistle and asked, "Do you think it was Jesus who made her well?"

"I do," replied Joseph of Arimathea. "I certainly do."

The two men walked on in silence.

As they headed toward the bakery, Joseph nudged Mathias and pointed to the crowded eatery.

"Business is good, my friend," stated Joseph.

"I was quite certain it would be," said Mathias in response. "Oh! I must order a delivery of water for Simon's baking." Mathias suddenly recalled Simon's request from earlier that morning. "I almost forgot!" he said, putting his hand to his head.

As they passed the inn where they were staying, Mathias ducked in and spoke to the innkeeper. Together they made arrangements for a large crock of water to be brought to the Top Shelf. Mathias paid the owner and put an extra coin in the man's hand to compensate him for delivering the pitcher.

"Have it there by this afternoon," Mathias instructed.

The innkeeper assured him that the delivery would be made.

***

In Bethany, Jesus was reclining with Lazarus on the porch of the home where the once dead, now resurrected, man lived with his sisters, Mary and Martha. Martha brought out a cool fruit drink for the two men to enjoy, but it was clear that Jesus was distracted. He kept checking the sundial in the garden.

"Where are Simon Peter and John?" Jesus asked Martha.

"Out by the barn," she answered.

"Would you let them know it's time to go back into the city and prepare for the Passover meal?"

Martha leaned over the porch railing and called the two men. In a few moments, they sauntered up to the porch and grabbed their packs.

"We will be off then," Peter said.

"When you get to the city, you will see a man carrying water in a pot. Follow him to where he is going, and he will lead you to the place that I have chosen for our private dinner this night." Jesus was solemn as he dismissed the disciples.

The two men shook hands with the rabbi and with Lazarus.

"I will see you at dusk," Jesus's voice was tense but friendly.

"Where are they off to?" It was Judas who asked the question.

Jesus looked squarely back at Judas but did not answer him.

***

Peter and John entered the city of Jerusalem about an hour after they departed Bethany.

"Jesus told us to find a man carrying water and to follow him," reported John.

No sooner had he said the words, when a man came out of the inn carrying a large crock of water. He held it high up on his shoulder.

"Look!" Peter said.

"Should we follow him?" queried John.

"I think we had better!" came Peter's response.

As they walked behind the man, they couldn't help but notice that they were on the same block as the Top Shelf Bakery. They then watched as the man turned and went down the alley that ran parallel to the west side of the bakery.

"We are to eat here tonight?" Peter mouthed the words in disbelief.

Sure enough, Simon of Cyrene appeared at the delivery door and received the water from the man who had brought it to him. Looking down the alley, he saw the two disciples standing in the street.

"Just in time!" Simon called to the pair. "I have just taken the rolls out of the oven, and the unleavened bread is ready as well. Come in, come in."

Peter and John dutifully followed Simon into the rear of the bakery. Once inside, John asked Simon a question. "I know you have made food provisions for our Passover meal tonight, but I need to ask you, do you have room for us to dine here as well?"

Simon nodded his head and smiled. Then he said, "Follow me."

The trio went up the backstairs to the second floor where they entered a large upper room.

"I plan to utilize this room for banquets and special occasions, but it's unused for now."

"It's perfect," said John.

Simon left the two men upstairs and went back down to the kitchen. The café was busy with the midday crowd, and Rufus was busy taking orders.

"Hey, Dad!" he called.

Rufus seemed so happy to be part of the bakery's success. He came over to his father and gave him a hug.

"We are doing it!" the young man exclaimed. "Open for business and making sales!"

"Indeed, we are," said Simon.

Peter and John came down the stairs and announced that the upper room was ready.

"Ready for what?" Rufus asked.

"It seems that Jesus will be dining here tonight, upstairs in the big room." Simon replied.

"Then I volunteer my services as head waiter," said Rufus, snapping to attention.

"Head waiter you shall be." Peter laughed. "But keep the food your father makes on hand, because I will be plenty hungry by dinner time."

"At your command!" saluted Rufus.

With that, the two disciples headed out to the street and into the bustling crowd. Rufus could not be certain, but he was quite sure he saw a man at the door to the Top Shelf give a wave and a hand signal to a small group of men on the corner. With a nod and another wave of his hand, the group began to follow the two disciples, keeping a safe distance between them so as not to be noticed.

The afternoon was busy as the patrons came by the score to sample the delicacies from Simon's kitchen. Rufus was fascinated by the representatives from different cultures who sat at the tables, many speaking in languages that he did not know. Jerusalem was packed with visitors from all over the world, pilgrims and tourists, many who made their way into the Top Shelf Bakery. Mathias was hosting, clearing tables, and seating guests. He was a natural at making visitors feel welcomed and appreciated. Little Cico did his part by chattering away and entertaining the patrons with his tricks and comical expressions.

As the day moved closer to the dinner hour, the crowd began to return to their homes and hotels. Rufus slipped the coins that he had received as payment throughout the day into Simon's money belt, and then began to blow out candles and extinguish lamps. Soon, the patrons made their way to the door and exited out onto the street. Mathias locked the door and looked at Rufus.

"Let's go upstairs and see if Jesus is here yet," he said softly.

"I thought I heard footsteps going up the back stairway a few moments ago."

Together, with Simon trailing behind, they ascended the narrow stairs and arrived on the second floor. Looking over the wooden railing, they saw Jesus and about a dozen or so of His followers. They were sitting around the large table, talking casually and laughing at appropriate junctures. At this moment, the one called Matthew was telling a humorous story, much to the delight of the rest of the group.

"Here are our hosts!" exclaimed John.

After handshakes and pleasantries were exchanged, Mathias said, "We will have dinner on the table in ten minutes."

With that, Rufus got busy running to and from the kitchen keeping plates and goblets full throughout the meal. Several times, Jesus nodded and thanked Rufus for his service. Rufus thought he would do anything for the miracle worker, but as evening turned to night, he couldn't help but notice a strange sorrow in Jesus's eyes that had not been there earlier.

After the meal had been finished and the conversation had grown quiet, Jesus asked Rufus to fill His cup and to bring Him a loaf of flatbread. Rufus placed the bread before the teacher and poured fresh wine with the large jug from the kitchen. As he handed the cup to Jesus, he smiled. Jesus looked tired, but He smiled back and placed His hand over Rufus's hand.

"Stay close to me now," said Jesus. "I want you to remember what is about to take place."

Jesus cleared His throat, and the chatter ceased. It was obvious that He was troubled.

"One of you is going to turn me in tonight," He said solemnly. "I feel sorrier for that one than I can tell you. He is plotting, even now, to hand me over to the temple guards."

"Is it me?" Simon Peter spoke first.

The others, sitting around the table, all asked the same question. "Me? Is it me?"

Jesus took the loaf of bread and broke it, passing half to those seated on His right and half to those seated on His left.

"Take a piece of this bread," He said, "and picture, as you tear it apart, that this will happen to me very soon. For this bread is like my body, being broken for you."

He then took the cup and passed it around the room, saying, "The wine goes down smoothly, but my blood will flow, and you will swallow hard, for I will soon die to seal the new agreement between heaven and earth."

After a lengthy pause, He continued, "Don't be afraid, my brothers. I love you and I am doing this for you and for many who will come after you."

Rufus stood in shock as he tried to take in what he had just heard. He felt overwhelmed and frightened. He took a few steps toward the stairs and then went down to the bottom step where he sat, alone with his head in his hands. He had not been there long when he heard footsteps above him. A man hurriedly brushed by and pushed Rufus out of the way, running past him into the night. Rufus was certain that it was the disciple known as Judas Iscariot.

Rufus didn't move for some time. Pictures flashed in his mind of the gladiator battles back at home in Cyrene. He thought of Thomas of Thera, lying in the dust and the blood that poured from his wounded body. Was something like that about to happen to Jesus? He could not bear the thought. He heard movement upstairs. Dinner was over, and the men were preparing to leave. One of them began singing a Jewish folk song. It was surely one the men knew well because their voices blended in harmony. Down the stairs they came with Jesus leading the way.

"Rufus, I cannot thank you enough for your service tonight." Jesus put His hand on the shoulder of Rufus and looked deep into his eyes. "Things are going to get pretty rough for a while," He said. "Don't be afraid, and never give way to doubt."

The group passed by Rufus as he stood at the door, each of them giving him a hearty handshake and a thank-you. They went out to the street, but before they were completely out of sight, Rufus closed the door behind him and went after them. It appeared as though they were headed for the Mount of Olives. Rufus followed at a distance. Jesus led them out the city gate, across the Kidron Valley, and into the park called Gethsemane. Rufus hid himself behind a small shack that was utilized to store pots and other equipment used for collecting olive oil. He did not know why he was so frightened, but he could not stop shaking. He wished he had brought his cloak to ward off the chill. He curled into a ball and waited. For what, he was unsure.

He did not know how long he had been sleeping when he awoke with a start. A mob carrying torches and weapons had entered the park. Rufus scrambled to his feet just in time to see Jesus and His disciples enter the clearing just beyond where He was hiding.

Jesus was saying, "They are here now. Get ready for the hardest night of your life."

Out of the dark, one man emerged into the clearing and stood before Jesus. "Have you decided better of it, Judas?"

Rufus gasped as he recognized Judas Iscariot who had left the upper room just hours before.

"Have you come back to join us?" Jesus asked the traitor. He then wiped His eyes as though He had been crying.

"You know why I am here, Teacher," replied Judas smugly.

With that, he leaned over and kissed Jesus on His cheek. "A kiss? You plan to betray me with a kiss, Judas?" Jesus asked.

"It is I who feel betrayed, Jesus," replied Judas. "I have followed you for years and would have marched by your side to take the throne from Rome. But you were unwilling to finish the job, and we remain powerless and at the mercy of Caesar. One last miracle would get the job done! But no, you leave us in the lurch without a rallying cry. I am going to force your hand and see what happens, but the revolution starts now!"

As Judas uttered those words, the angry mob stepped into the clearing.

"Grab him!" someone shouted.

"Why do you hunt me down like an animal?" Jesus said above the din. "Every day I taught in the temple courts, and you could have detained me at any time."

"You are Jesus of Nazareth, then?" asked one of the temple guards.

"I *am*," spoke Jesus, and as he said those words, Rufus saw the entire mob fall backward as if hit by a wave on the sea.

For a moment, Jesus stood alone.

Rufus could contain himself no longer. "Run, Jesus! Run away," he called, stepping out of hiding.

Just then, everything became chaos. Jesus did not run, but His disciples did. They scattered everywhere, running in all directions. Men with swords and clubs grabbed Jesus and bound His hands.

Rufus watched in horror as the mob gave chase to the fleeing disciples.

Peter ran past Rufus and shouted, "Get out of here! Run!"

He turned and began to run, only to trip on a tree root. He scrambled to his feet but too late. A man with a torch grabbed his tunic with his free hand. Rufus shed his shirt and ran into the night, his feet pounding the earth beneath him and his breath coming in gasps. He did not stop until he reached the inn. Running up the stairs to his room, he buried his face in his pillow and wept.

A Baker's Hands

Simon
"Jesus, I believe."

Judas stood in the hallway outside the room where the temple guard had brought Jesus. He had never heard anything like what was happening inside the conference room. Men were screaming obscenities. They were trying to trap Jesus into admitting He was a phony. They shouted that his authority to produce miracles was from the prince of darkness and not heaven. Whenever the door opened to allow someone to enter or to exit the room, Judas would strain to see inside. What he saw, sickened him. Jesus's hands were tied behind him, and a burlap bag had been thrown over his head. He was completely defenseless as men took turns punching him in the face or clubbing him with sticks on his neck and shoulders.

"Tell us who it was who hit you," they cackled.

Judas felt his own heart pounding in his chest. Unable to watch any longer, he ran from the temple and hid himself in a tavern where he ordered a bottle of cheap wine. It was obvious. Now that the religious leaders had Jesus in custody, they were planning to do more than lock Him up for a few days.

"They want Him dead," Judas said aloud.

He put his head down on the table where he sat and moaned. Suddenly he sat up as if he had realized something. He jumped to his feet and ran back to the temple. The room where they had been questioning Jesus was now empty. A servant was inside, cleaning up the mess and straightening out the furniture.

"Where did they take him?" Judas demanded.

Before the servant could answer, a priest appeared in the doorway. "Ah! Judas," said the priest, "you have done us a great service this night. They have taken the prisoner to Pilate for a formal pronouncement of treason. That man, Jesus claims He is a king."

"You were just supposed to lock him up for a few days," Judas exclaimed. "He is not guilty of anything, and you want to have him killed as a traitor!"

"He is our problem now," said the priest in a pious tone. "You did your part."

"Well, I want to undo it!" Judas was close to tears.

"I am afraid that's not possible," stated the priest, and he turned and walked away.

He cringed suddenly as a bag of money hit the wall by his head, breaking open and sending thirty silver coins rattling down the hallway. He turned to look, but Judas was gone.

***

Across the temple courtyard, but more than a world away, Rufus slowly awakened. He could see Joseph and Mathias in conversation in the adjacent room.

"Good morning, Rufus," said Uncle Mat. "By the looks of it, you had quite a night." He was looking at Rufus's feet. They were filthy and scratched.

"So it wasn't a bad dream," the young Cyrenian managed to say.

Over the next few minutes, Rufus shared what he had witnessed in Gethsemane.

"So Judas sold him out," said Mathias.

Joseph then shared what he had seen in the temple and at Pilate's palace. "They sent Jesus to Herod, and he refused to get involved," continued Joseph. "He is back at Pilate's headquarters now, and he is to be tried publicly this morning. A crowd is already gathering."

The men went to the window that overlooked the courtyard, and there they could see groups of people mingling in anticipation.

"Where is my dad?" Rufus directed the question at his uncle.

"He's at the bakery," said Mathias. "He said for you to come help him when you awoke."

"I had better wash up first," Rufus replied.

"Put on something clean," Mathias said flatly. "Joseph and I will go to the courtyard. We will let you know what happens."

Rufus so wanted to go with the two men; however, he knew his father needed him at the bakery. He donned a clean tunic after bathing and headed for the Top Shelf Bakery. In a few minutes, he entered the kitchen and said good morning to his dad. Simon was glad to see his son.

"The upper room has not been cleared or cleaned," he said to Rufus. "Would you start collecting plates and cups and wash them?"

Rufus turned and ran up the stairway to the room where Jesus had dined last evening. It hardly seemed possible that he was now under arrest.

Rufus went about his task of clearing dishes. He picked up the goblet that he had filled for Jesus the previous evening and kept it separate from the rest. He wasn't sure why, but he wanted to save this cup that had been so solemnly passed around the table. He wrapped it in a cloth and put it in his pack. Later, he would bring it to his room, but for now, he was simply glad to have it. Somehow, it made him feel like Jesus was with him.

An hour or so later, Mathias returned to the Top Shelf alone. He looked pale. His eyes were red from crying.

"Joseph is meeting with the Sanhedrin," he said with his head in his hands. "They got what they wanted. They are going to crucify Jesus. They paid off Pilate and released some prisoner named Barabbas in exchange for the death penalty for Jesus."

Mathias swallowed hard and went on. "It was a contrived arrangement from the start. The temple guards were pouring wine from huge wineskins into cups and crocks, whatever they could find, and offered it freely to every low life that hung around the courtyard. They instructed these men to call for the release of Barabbas when Pilate requested a vote. They said that Barabbas was a brave patriot and that he was needed in the growing ranks of anti-Roman sentiment. They swayed the crowd, and sure enough, they demanded that Jesus be put to death. They tied him to the whipping post and tore him apart. He was covered in blood when they dragged him away and threw him into a prison cell. Within the hour, he will be brought outside the city gates, and there they will kill him. It's a horrible thing that has happened."

Rufus ran. He did not know where to run to, but he felt frightened and sad, and so he put his head down and ran. He felt emotions much like those he did on the day that Thomas of Thera lay dying in the arena back in Cyrene. He thought of home and Celine, his mother. How far from him now they both seemed. It seemed crazy, but he wished he could not stop running until he was safe at home again.

His feet slapped the street as he ran past the markets and through the temple courts. As he pushed his way through the throng, he stumbled and crashed into a man headed in the opposite direction. The force of the collision nearly knocked him off his feet. Immediately he recognized the man as Judas Iscariot, one of the twelve. Judas seemed to recognize Rufus as well. He said nothing. Instead, he placed his hand on Rufus and whispered just two words.

"Forgive me." He then turned away and was gone, disappearing into the sea of people.

***

Back at the bakery, Simon and Mathias were worried about Rufus.

"I have got to go find him," Simon stated while pacing the floor of the kitchen.

"He could be anywhere out there. Mathias, will you watch the shop while I go find my boy?"'

"Go!" said Mathias. "And may God go with you."

Simon stopped and looked at Mathias. "I don't believe as you do, Mathias," said Simon flatly. "God has left us here on our own," he muttered. "If there even is a god."

With that, he headed out to the street. He moved east toward the temple, searching the crowd and calling for Rufus.

***

Meanwhile, Rufus ran. His eyes were too full of tears to see well where he was going, and so he slowed his pace and followed the crowd. In the midst of the throng, he felt lost. He was in a part of Jerusalem that he had not seen yet. The streets narrowed and were lined with shops and apartments. He could see the huge gate that led out of the city to Gehenna, the garbage dump. Smoke rose from the fires that burned day and night, and the breeze brought the smell of rot to Rufus's nostrils. He left the crowd that had slowed to a stop at the markets and headed east down a winding street that was empty of traffic. Just then, Rufus saw why the street was deserted. A wedge of Roman soldiers was clearing the way for a pitiful sight. No one was allowed near the slow-moving entourage. A bloodied figure was straining under the weight of a wooden cross, trying to keep pace with the soldiers. He was being forced to carry the heavy crossbeam alone. Rufus quickly hid himself behind a column and waited for the scene to pass by him. As the soldiers drew close, Rufus could clearly see the man with the cross on his back. He knew who it was, but his heart would not let him believe it. Swollen and soaked in blood, the man was not recognizable. Rufus stepped out of hiding to get a closer look. Just at that moment, the man under the crushing weight looked over at Rufus. Their eyes met, and Rufus could not hold back his heart.

"Jesus!" he screamed, and he ran to the middle of the street where the exhausted man had fallen.

"Get off him, boy!" a centurion barked the order.

With his long staff, he hit Rufus in the ribs, and for a minute, Rufus could barely breathe. Nonetheless, he managed to help Jesus of Nazareth to His knees and then tried to shoulder the heavy burden of the massive wooden beam. Try as he might, Rufus could not lift the cross.

Jesus was exhausted and in agony, yet He managed to smile at Rufus. "A blessing on you, young Rufus," He said through his parched lips.

"Why are they doing this to you?" Rufus searched the face of Jesus for an answer.

"No one takes my life from me," Jesus replied. He moaned as a centurion laid a whip to His back.

"Get up!" the soldier bellowed.

"I willingly lay my life down so to offer forgiveness for many," Jesus spoke deliberately in a hoarse voice.

"I do not understand!" cried Rufus.

"We will see each other again, Rufus," Jesus stated. "Then you will know what occurred here on this day."

"Rufus!" Simon's voice came clearly over the noise of the crowd. "What are you doing, my son?"

"Oh, Father… Look what they have done to Jesus," Rufus said as he rushed to his father's arms. "We must help him!"

Simon tried to comprehend the scene before him. As he witnessed the cruelty and horror, he was suddenly seized by a compassion that he had never known. He pushed past his son and the soldiers and pulled Jesus to His feet.

"I will help you, Jesus," whispered Simon.

He shouldered the heavy wood and struggled to stand under the weight. Deep splinters pierced his baker's hands as the line began to move toward the city gate and the burning dump called Gehenna.

LIFE AND DEATH

Simon and Jesus
"I will help you Jesus."

Simon stumbled into the Top Shelf Bakery with Rufus right beside him. His arms and hands were bloodied, and his knees were scraped raw.

"What happened to you?" Mathias asked as he rushed to sit Simon down in the kitchen.

Simon was too exhausted to talk. He managed to whisper to his brother-in-law that he had tried to carry the cross that they used to crucify Jesus, but his words made little sense. Rufus hushed his father and applied warm, wet cloths to the gashes on his torso.

"He tried to help ease the weight of the wooden beam that Jesus was forced to carry to the hill of the skull," Rufus explained. "Father carried it to the city gate and then dropped it, but then the Romans made him pick it up and carry it to the top of the hill. Jesus took one end, and Father took the other, but five men would have struggled under such a burden."

"How did you get involved with this?" Mathias asked Simon.

"It was my fault," Rufus interjected. "I happened to see the line of soldiers coming up the street. Then I saw Jesus stumble under the weight he was trying to carry, so I ran to help him. That is where I was when Father found me. He stepped in and tried to help us both, but the soldiers made him help carry the load. He protested saying he was not an Israelite so he could not be conscripted by Rome, but when they asked him where he was from, he told them Cyrene, which they maintained was a Roman colony. That meant he was under their jurisdiction. They threatened to imprison him if he didn't comply."

Rufus stopped and wiped his eyes.

"It sounds horrible," Mathias said in a low voice.

"That's not the worst part," Rufus continued. "They got to the top of Skull Hill, and they nailed Jesus to the cross. Then they shoved the post into a hole and raised Him up. He is hanging there now. I left to bring Father back here. Jesus has been hanging on that cross for hours now."

***

Joseph of Arimathea had left the scene of death and suffering, and as he strode down the path, past the burning fires of the municipal dump, he remembered a time that now seemed long ago… Many years after Jesus was crucified, he shared the story with Mathias in a letter. It read…

> *I recall, the salt spray was blinding as the wind battered the groaning ship. I shielded my eyes and scanned the main deck. We were riding very low in the water, our hold below, full of a rich haul of*

ore from the tin mines of Britannia. The wind was driving us ahead in the full onslaught of the storm, and the boat was in present danger of going under, there could be no doubt. I, Joseph, had often made this run, but this time, I was especially concerned. I had onboard more than just a cargo of raw tin. This time I had my niece Mary and her thirteen-year-old son Jesus Bar-Joseph on board the freighter. Mary, recently widowed, had agreed to go on the journey to assist me, and young Jesus had come aboard for his first real job as a cabin boy.

I had thought the change of scenery and the adventure of the boundless sea would do Mary and Jesus some good. Mary's husband had passed away just four months before. The family had been settled in Nazareth where Joseph labored as a less than successful woodworker, always struggling to overcome public ridicule. Years before, prior to his marriage to Mary, the carpenter had claimed to have been visited by angels in a dream. He asserted that Jesus was not his actual son, but was a king, God in the flesh.

"Rome has little time left to oppress us," he was known to say. "Our Jesus will become a mighty king and lead the nation to freedom." The local townsfolk considered him crazy, and though his work was first-rate, his customers were few. He passed away quite suddenly, leaving Mary alone to find work to support the family. As her uncle, I had thought the merchant trip to Britannia would be a good distraction for Mary, and I promised to pay her to serve as cook aboard ship. Jesus had signed on to assist his mother.

"We may have to jettison some of the load!" The cry of the first mate came over the howling wind.

"I don't like this one bit," I called back, pointing to the waves breaking over the hull.

"We are riding too low in the waves," the crew member warned. "Any one of these breakers could swamp us and take us to the bottom!"

"If that occurs, we will likely all perish. We are miles and miles from any land, and the sea is very cold."

The weather was now growing even more fierce, drowning out our voices under the horrible whining of wind and wood.

I was about to call out "All hands on deck!" in an effort to assemble the crew and begin the dangerous task of lightening the ship's cargo when suddenly, everything stopped.

The wind instantly changed to a fair and gentle breeze. The sun appeared high in the sky, and the angry waves ceased their battering of the vessel, instead becoming calm and quiet as they gently lapped the sides of the boat. My first mate let out a low whistle.

"What just happened?" His voice quivered as he asked me the question.

I responded with a nod toward the bow of the boat. There stood the young Jesus, arms extended, His head turned toward heaven. Just as I was about to call out to Jesus, the young lad turned and looked directly into my eyes. His face, framed by His long wet hair, broke into a broad grin. He hopped down off the rolled canvas sail He was perched upon and walked past the stymied crew.

His face grew solemn. He paused as if weighing his thoughts. "Before too long, it will be my turn to face a storm angrier than this one today," Jesus stated matter-of-factly.

He looked deep into my eyes.

"It will require your own bravery and courage. On that day, remember this one. I will be with you always, I promise."

"Did you just... Was it you who... The wind and waves...gone? We were about to die!" I remember struggling for words.

Jesus put His finger to my lips. "Just remember what has occurred," the young man said earnestly. "There is something more powerful than death."

This story is true.

Signed,
Joseph, your friend and brother in the faith

***

Some two decades later, Joseph buttressed himself against another howling gale as he walked the narrow path from Golgotha, just outside of Jerusalem. His nephew, Jesus was hanging dead on a Roman cross behind him, atop the rugged hill. Joseph was on his way to the temple to bargain with the Romans for the body of Jesus.

Moments later, a crack of thunder split the sky as the wind moaned through the columns of the portico. But Joseph's thoughts were back some twenty years earlier, on board a sinking ship in the middle of the Great Sea. He recalled the immediate calm that silenced that storm. He recalled the words that the young Jesus had told him to remember.

"I will be with you always, I promise."

The peace that conquered an ocean gale now conquered Joseph's own troubled heart. It was inside of him.

"I remember," the tin merchant said aloud. "In fact, I shall never forget. I am but a battered, sinking vessel in the boundless ocean of heaven's peace. And you, Jesus, are forever my captain, the only One who is stronger than death itself."

***

As Jesus hung on the cross, so eternity hung in the balance...

***

"What was that?" Mathias ran to the doorway of the Top Shelf Bakery and looked outside. There at the door, he met Joseph who had planned to stop into the bakery on his way to see Pilate.

Just then, a rumble within the earth seemed to come up from beneath them. It grew in intensity as it began to shake buildings and trees.

"Earthquake!" yelled Mathias.

Rufus was thrown across the kitchen and up against the wall at the back of the room. He could see his father lying on the floor, covered in plaster and dust. Mathias was shielding him with his body as the building swayed like a ship at sea. Suddenly he could see nothing. A thick darkness settled over the eatery. Like the blackness of a deep well, the sudden gloom was so intense that you could not see your hand in front of your face. Then, just as suddenly as it began, the shaking of the earth ceased. All was quiet.

"Rufus?" Mathias's voice called to him through the pitch blackness.

"Here, Uncle Mat," Rufus answered him. "I'm okay."

"I don't understand the sudden night that has befallen us," Mathias stated. "It seems to be over all of Jerusalem, for I can see nothing outside."

The three men did not move from their places for some time. Before long, the tap, tap of rain on the roof could be heard. Rufus shivered as crackling thunder boomed over the city. The oncoming storm sent flashes of lightning across the jet-black sky, allowing a few seconds of light to illuminate the dark kitchen. Rufus strained his eyes to see, but the darkness was too thick. He could see nothing. The wind began to howl, and the rain began to pour in torrents.

"What a storm," Mathias shouted above the gale.

"Are you okay, Father?" Rufus shouted into the dark.

"I am all right," Simon called back.

And then, just as quickly as it began, the violent storm ceased. Light began to return to the sky. Simon slowly rose to his feet. "I am telling you," he said. "Jesus is no ordinary man. And this was no ordinary day."

"A very unusual storm as well," Mathias observed.

Later, after order had been restored in the bakery, Joseph of Arimathea entered the store. He had a distinguished-looking man with him, whose clothing was that of an elder, but whose face seemed ageless. Not a line nor a wrinkle was to be found on him.

"Gentlemen, I have two amazing things to tell you," he began. "One is this: a half-hour ago, the curtain in the temple, you know the thick one that covers the most holy place, well, it was destroyed. It was ripped in two as if a giant pair of hands ripped it down the middle. The most incredible part is that it tore from top to bottom!"

The trio of Rufus, Simon, and Mathias tried to take in what Joseph was saying. No human could have ripped that veil which blocked the entrance to the holy of holies.

"I have one other thing to tell you," continued Joseph. "I buried my father some fifteen years ago. But, gentlemen, it is with great pleasure and true wonder that I introduce you now to Samuel of Arimathea, my father. I recognized him about an hour ago at the temple. There were others there whom I also remembered as having been dead and buried for years. Who can explain this to me?"

Mathias and Rufus shook hands with Samuel and invited him in to sit down.

"I cannot stay," replied the gentleman. "Something calls to me from the land beyond. I will be departing soon, but I am here now, and I want to assure you that all of heaven's angels are focused on this day and this city. It is an historical moment."

Having spoken, Joseph's father stood up and bid the men goodbye. He exited the bakery and entered the busy street, and then he was no more.

"My family grave lies empty," Joseph said in a hushed tone. With that, he slipped out the door and headed up the street. He was on his way to the governor's palace with a noble but heart-wrenching job to do. Back in the bakery, the room was silent for a time as each individual tried to comprehend the events of the day. It was Simon who broke the silence.

"He sang to me," Simon said weakly.

"Who?" Mathias questioned. "Who sang to you?"

"Jesus did," replied Simon. "On the way up Skull Hill. We were trying desperately to haul that heavy beam to the crest of the hill. It was muddy and slippery, and we could not keep our footing. At one point, Jesus turned to me and said, 'Thank you.' The Roman guard punched me, hard in my chest. I struggled just to breathe while the soldier said there was to be no talking to the prisoners. Just at that moment, Jesus started singing to me as we made our way up the hill. The words were beautiful. I can recall them even now."

He built his sanctuary
like the heights on Mt. Zion
like the earth that he established forever.
He chose his servant
and took him from the flocks and fields;
from tending the sheep, he brought him
to be the shepherd of his people,
of Israel his inheritance.
And David shepherded them
with integrity of heart;
with skillful hands he led them.

"He kept on singing—even as they drove spikes into his wrists and fastened him to the beam we had carried. His eyes flowed with tears. He must have been in agony. When he could no longer sing, he hummed the melody. As they raised him off the ground, I heard him asking his Father to forgive the ones who were torturing him for they did not know he was sent from heaven."

"Do you now believe that he was?" Mathias looked into Simon's eyes as he asked the question.

"I don't know," Simon replied. "I am beginning to believe. I reason that much is true."

The three men sat alone in the Top Shelf and tried to comprehend what the day had brought them. A knock on the back door by the kitchen suddenly scattered their thoughts. It was Peter, and he looked like he'd seen a ghost.

"Peter! Come in, come in," Mathias took him by the arm and gave him a hug. "You are shaking, my friend."

Peter was a rugged fisherman and not much could rattle him. But he was clearly undone and desperate as he entered the bakery.

"Jesus is dead," Peter gasped out the words.

He sat down on a stool and tried to gather himself.

"I was afraid to get too close to the execution, so I hung back in the crowd. I could not hear anything, and I didn't want to see much. But Mary, his mother, was struggling to get his body off the cross before sundown. I went to her and offered my help. She didn't seem to hear me. Her body was shaking, and her desperate wailing drowned out all the noise around her. Joseph said that he would take care of the body. He had permission from Pilate to place Jesus in his family burial site. He wants to bring him here now and prepare him for burial. He sent me ahead to ask you to put jugs of water and a white linen cloth upstairs. We must have him buried by sundown."

At that moment, John came to the door. On his back was a hideous sight. He carried the lifeless Jesus in out of the rain. He was followed by two women.

"Simon, these women wish to thank you for your generosity," said Joseph in a voice no louder than a whisper.

They are Mary of Magdala and Mary the mother of Jesus.

Simon felt awkward but managed to say, "We are sorry for your loss."

The elder Mary nodded at Simon and smiled at Rufus despite her tears. She seemed so very noble but very tired. She leaned toward John and whispered something in his ear. John pointed to the stairs.

"We won't be long," said John. "But we must hurry."

He then went upstairs, still shouldering his burden. He rolled the lifeless body of Jesus off his shoulders and onto the big table where he and the two Marys began washing his bruised and bloodied frame. Rufus stood and watched from the corner of the room. As Mary, the mother of Jesus stood by the body of her dead son, she was lost in a world of her own thoughts. Tears coursed down her face as she tried to comprehend the loss. It had been such a joy to raise him, even after Joseph passed away. He was obedient and thoughtful. He was kind and helpful. Now he was dead.

In the earlier years, when Jesus was a boy, she had often been ridiculed for her "angel story," as the locals referred to it. They were certain it was just a fanciful tale, meant to cover her obvious indiscretion. Pregnant out of wedlock, she was not the first such girl in Nazareth to end up in this type of trouble… But to say that God had fathered the child was unthinkable, and her neighbors let her know it. Many nights she tried to sleep with the echo of scornful words still playing in her head. Maybe it had all been a dream. Perhaps there had never been any angels. Maybe she had been sick with a fever and imagined the vision of Gabriel, her heavenly visitor. She shook her head to clear her thoughts. On nights such as these, she would sometimes get up and go peek at the sleeping boy in the next room. She knew he was different…destined to be the king. The angel had told her that.

"Just wait," she would say under her breath. "They will see soon enough."

But then her son had changed. As an adult, He began to befriend fishermen and tax collectors, harlots and thieves. Hardly heroes. She had pleaded with Him to take time away and to remember His calling. But He had not listened. He was at odds with the Sanhedrin—not one of them. Now, no one would ever think of Him as special. The lie she had been accused of would be confirmed in the public opinion. She had heard it already at the cross that very day.

"I thought you said He was going to be a king!" a pharisee hollered that in her direction. "Tell Him to come down, and we will make Him king!" Their venom was appalling.

Now His lifeless body lay before her. She knew nothing more to do than to bury him. And she did know one other thing. She had loved him.

When they had finished their grim task, the two women brought out some ointment and told Simon to sit down. They rubbed the balm into Simon's wounds.

"I heard you performed an act of kindness for my son today," Mary spoke quietly. "I am most grateful. May you and your own son be blessed."

She broke down again at those words and began to weep uncontrollably.

"This is not what the angel promised…" She held her head in her hands. "My son was to be a king. Now look at him. Where did I fail?"

"Oh, Mary, you did not fail." It was the other Mary who spoke. "This tragedy is not your fault."

"It must be," replied the older woman. "His father has been gone for years now. It was my responsibility to guide him into his destiny the angel spoke of. God chose me to raise him and I failed." Her shoulders shook, and her tears fell to the floor.

"Mary, I will take him now," Joseph said. "I will place him in my own family tomb. We must go now as the sun is low in the sky."

Mathias wrapped the body in the linen cloth, and together he and Rufus carried Jesus down the stairs and out the door. There Joseph and his friend Nicodemus of the Sanhedrin took the body and headed out the city gate to the grave where they would lay him. John left for his home, taking Mary with him. Mary of Magdala stayed behind and, together with Rufus, cleaned the table and floor of the upper room.

The men arrived at the sepulcher just as the sun was setting. There they placed the lifeless body of Jesus in the crypt and rolled a large cut stone in front of the opening. They stood in silence outside the tomb. Minutes passed. Finally, Joseph spoke.

"I don't think I can imagine life without him," he said in a hushed tone.

Nicodemus nodded. "I am certain that I will have lost my position in the synagogue, although I don't mind after seeing how those men behaved like jackals."

"I am leaving Jerusalem in a short while," Joseph said sadly. "I need to get away." He wiped his nose on his sleeve but could not hide his tears.

The two men heard footsteps and saw torchlights coming up to the small clearing in front of the grave. Joseph and Nicodemus stood unseen in the shadow of the trees. Into the glade stepped a group of ten Roman military men, in full battle gear. The elder Nicodemus and Joseph quickly ran down a small path that led away from the site. One soldier heard their footsteps on the path and gave chase. After just a few strides, he stopped and called into the darkness, "Who goes there?" Nicodemus and Joseph did not slow their pace.

As they came out to the main road, they heard the soldier's voice in the distance, warning, "Don't come up here again. We have posted a guard and are sealing this tomb with the mark of Caesar on orders from the governor."

"Caiaphas must be plenty worried that someone will steal the body of Jesus and claim that he is alive," Joseph said, his words coming in gasps. "Since the story of Lazarus has gotten around, many people are half-expecting Jesus to be stronger than death itself. If they find out where he is buried, they may secretly take the corpse and put up a lookalike in his stead. Such a move could set a revolt in motion. The leadership in the temple will lose their influence. Jesus could present a bigger problem to them now that he is dead than he did while he was alive."

The pair walked back through the city gate and headed for the bakery. There was a lone light in the window, so Joseph ran up to the doorway and knocked. To his surprise, Matthew answered the door and quickly ushered them in.

"There's talk of arresting us," Matthew hissed. "They want to keep us from stealing the body, and they figure we can't accomplish that if we are locked up."

Simon and Rufus joined the conversation.

"You can lay low here in the upstairs room," Simon spoke quietly. "I told Matthew and the others no one would think that you were still in Jerusalem. They will be looking out in Bethany and beyond."

"We could not move the body if we wanted to," Nicodemus shot back. "Pilate has placed soldiers at the grave. We saw them!"

"Apparently the entrance has been sealed with Caesar's inscription," Joseph added.

"No one is taking any chances, and neither should we," continued the elder gentleman. "I say that the upper room here will be a logical place to stay secretive."

Over the next few hours, more of the disciples of Jesus found their way to the upper room at Simon's bakery. John brought Mary, the mother of their dead leader.

"I don't want to be alone," Mary remarked to Mathias. "I want to be with the people who knew my son, with his friends."

Martha, the sister of Lazarus, busied herself in the kitchen with Rufus while Simon napped in the dimly lit corner. Together they put a meal together for the men. No one felt much like eating, especially when Mary of Magdala brought news of Judas's death. He had taken his own life, she told them. The temple priests had buried the body before sundown. No one felt like talking. Tears were the only language in the upper room as the hours slipped by.

The Sabbath dawned, and with it came more fear and gloom. Rufus brought a tray of warm, kosher items, fresh from the oven, upstairs to Peter, who passed them out to the others. About midday, the two Marys quietly slipped out of the upper room and went down the back staircase to the street. They were intent on finding the tomb where Jesus was buried. Their plan was to wait for the Sabbath to pass and then plead with the guards to allow them to properly anoint the body of Jesus on Sunday. They were unsure as to whether or not they would be allowed access to the grave but considered it worth a try. Entering the garden where Joseph's sepulcher was being guarded, they approached the Roman soldiers who were posted around the sealed entrance to the grave. Through the night hours, they had pushed more large rocks up against the entrance. They were taking no chances—and said so.

"No, not a chance," the Roman centurion in charge of the soldiers said in such a matter-of-fact fashion that the two women knew there was no likelihood he would change his mind.

"I have orders from Pilate himself," stated the officer. "No one goes in. No one comes out."

He spoke with no expression on his face, however as he uttered those words, a low rumble of distant thunder could be heard rolling in over the Mount of Olives.

"Not another storm," said the Roman official.

Mary could see that he was a bit unnerved by the sound.

***

Back at the Top Shelf, Rufus stepped outside to look at the sky. He too had heard the sound of a brewing storm. Something was making him anxious and uneasy, and he knew it had nothing to do with the oncoming stormy weather. But what it was, he could not say. It was an excitement and anticipation in his spirit that defied logic. As the first large raindrops hit the dust at his feet, Rufus turned his face upward and let the rain fall on him. He let his tears flow with the rain. He realized how exhausted he was as a deep fatigue settled over him. He fell asleep to the sound of the rain. It was though the earth itself were crying. Not long after he fell asleep, Uncle Mathias carried him inside and lay him on a mat in the kitchen.

He awoke to the sound of pounding on the front door of the bakery. Rufus opened his eyes, and for a moment, he wondered where he was. The sun came brightly through the open kitchen windows, and a gentle breeze tossed his curls against his forehead. He sat up with a start as the sound of the fists upon the doorway brought his mind into focus. It was morning so that meant he had slept through the night on the kitchen floor. He looked outside to see the source of the banging at the Top Shelf front door. The sadness that had pushed him exhausted and into sleep suddenly returned as he recalled the horror of Friday and the sorrow of the sabbath. Now it was the first day of the week, and Rufus feared that the commotion meant that the Romans had come to arrest the disciples who were upstairs, apparently still asleep.

"Rufus! Open the door! Let us in!" The voice was a woman's voice.

Curious, Rufus looked out a small window next to the doorway only to see Mary the Magdalene and Mary the mother of Jesus outside the locked door. They were wide-eyed with excitement, and their voices were choked with tears. Rufus unlocked the door, and the two women pushed their way into the bakery.

"What's wrong?" Rufus asked.

"What's wrong?" the women answered. "Everything is all right! We just saw Jesus!"

"They opened the tomb for you?" Rufus was trying to understand their obvious joy.

"We don't know who opened it," cried Mary Magdalene. "But he wasn't in it!"

"Who wasn't in where?" Peter appeared at the foot of the stairs, followed by John. "What's going on?"

The women began to tell their story—how they had gone to the tomb before sunrise to see if they could convince the Roman guard to let them put spices in the grave. "But there were no soldiers…just two men sitting on the stone that had been placed at the mouth of the cave." The elder Mary was about out of breath, but she went on. "The grave was empty, so we thought the Romans had taken him away, but then, there he was, right before us—alive! He spoke to us. It was really him!"

Peter and John didn't say a word. They ran out the door and into the street, their feet pounding the pave stones as they hurried to the tomb. The women and Rufus dashed up the stairs where everyone was now awake.

"Impossible," said Matthew as the women told their story once again.

"I don't believe you," said another.

The more the women tried to explain, the more frustrated they became.

"Your mind is playing tricks on you," said the one called Thomas.

"Perhaps not," said Peter who had returned unnoticed along with John. Both men stood quietly at the top of the stairs.

Peter was holding a white linen cloth.

"This is the shroud we wrapped him with," he said reverently. "It was the only thing we found at the grave."

A loud discussion became an argument as the group debated whether or not the women's testimony of seeing Jesus alive and, well, could be believed. Was it actual or simply a combination of hysteria and exhaustion? Deciding to see for themselves, they hurried downstairs and out the door. Noticing that the disciples had left the linen cloth that had covered the dead body of Jesus, lying on the table, Rufus gathered it up, folded it neatly, and put it in his shoulder bag.

Mathias burst into the Top Shelf with a wide smile on his face. He summoned Rufus and Simon to the kitchen, waving his arms impatiently.

"Hurry up!" he called.

As soon as the three of them were together in the same room, Uncle Mat took a deep breath and said, "I just now saw Jesus!"

"Where?" asked Rufus and Simon in unison.

"In the temple courtyard. There had to be several others who saw him."

"Are you sure it was Jesus?" Simon asked the obvious question.

"There were holes in his wrists where the spikes had pierced him, and his feet bore the spike imprints also… It's Jesus all right. Our friend Joseph of Arimathea is by his side, testifying that he put a dead man in the grave on Friday and that this same man came out of the tomb this morning—alive!"

"Mary saw him too!" Simon winced as he stood to his feet. "She ran here to tell the others that Jesus spoke to her!"

"The men were skeptical, to say the least. They are all out investigating the tomb, even now."

With that, Mathias went to the window and looked toward the courtyard of the temple. He could see a crowd forming.

"This is amazing!" he whispered. "We saw his dead body upstairs just a few days ago. He was in a sealed grave. And yet now he is seen in the courtyard of the temple. It would appear that Jesus lives…"

Mathias sat down at a table and rubbed his face with his hands. "I thought we were coming to Jerusalem to build a business. Never did I dream that we would encounter events, such as we have, since we arrived. I think there was a bigger purpose in our coming here."

Simon and Rufus nodded in agreement. "I believe we were destined to meet Jesus."

By nightfall, the upper room was packed to the rafters. One of those in attendance was a Roman soldier who had been assigned to guard the tomb of Jesus. He captivated everyone in the room with his tale of what had occurred early Sunday morning. He described the air becoming thick with music as angels ascended and descended from the predawn sky. He shared how he and the other soldiers could not move. He spoke of the explosion of thunder and lighting and how the stone burst off the stone track it laid in. Then, there stood Jesus, surrounded by hundreds of glorious angels. The light was dazzling, and they had to look away. They were awestruck and fearful, and so they ran. They ran all the way to Pilate's palace where the governor was hosting his new friend, Herod Antipas. The two had formed an alliance over the past three days, and they seemed to revel in their mutual dismissal of the Jesus case. The Roman guards ran past the soldiers at the door and barged into the sleeping quarters where Pilate was just waking up with a painful hangover. King Herod was still asleep in the guest room. Snapping to attention, they all began to talk at once. Together they tripped over their words as they tried to communicate what had happened. Pilate, confused, annoyed and very angry, sent at once for Caiaphas.

"Wake the old buzzard if you must. Just bring him to me."

The disciples chuckled at those words.

"Did he really call him an old buzzard?" The question was out of Rufus's mouth before he realized it, which produced more laughter in the room.

The Roman went on, stating how Caiaphas showed up in his night robe and then how he and the temple officers had offered them a large sum of money if they would lie and make up a story about falling asleep while Jesus's followers stole the body. The soldiers refused to change their story. Pilate wanted to end this, so he ordered the immediate execution of the squad leader and threatened the rest of the troupe with the same sentence if they spoke a word to anyone. Rufus listened with rapt attention as the Roman wept aloud and struggled to finish his story. He said he would give up everything he owned now to follow Jesus. With that, the disciples, still cautious, welcomed him in. Despite the terror of the last several days, an uncertain joy seemed to permeate the room. Whenever someone mentioned Caiaphas appearing before Pilate in his nightshirt, the whole gathering laughed aloud.

Suddenly the laughter stopped and was replaced by an awed silence as each person's attention focused on a figure standing at the top of the stairs. No one had heard him come in.

It was Jesus. He did not appear haggard and beaten as He was on the cross. No, He was whole and strong and very much alive. He stretched out His arms in welcome, but no one dared to go near Him. The occupants of the upper room were beyond terrified.

"A ghost!" someone said.

Jesus went around the room and spoke earnestly to each one. He showed the holes in his hands and feet. He urged them to touch Him so that they could know He was flesh and blood, not a spirit. Slowly, acceptance replaced doubt, and love chased away fear.

"Can a man get some food in this fine establishment?" Jesus was apparently hungry.

Rufus ran to the kitchen and brought back a piece of broiled fish.

Jesus ate it in hearty fashion, savoring every bite.

"Not eating for three days makes one hungry," said Jesus with a nod toward the kitchen.

Rufus scurried back down the stairs and soon returned with more fish, some small cakes, and strawberry jam. The sadness of the last three days was gone. Jesus was alive. No one knew how it was possible, but they had seen Him with their own eyes and could not deny it.

WONDER AND WOE

The Top Shelf Bakery, Jerusalem
"The Top Shelf Bakery, which was now their favorite place to meet together."

The next weeks were filled with wonder. Jesus was no longer burdened and heavy hearted. He was joyful and playful—as if a huge weight had been taken off his shoulders. He smiled often. He made frequent stops at the Top Shelf, and there he spoke at length with Rufus. Mathias was absent from the bakery much of the time. He had left everything behind and now followed Jesus wherever he went. The other disciples loved Mathias's easy manner and his boisterous laugh. When it came time for the group to select a replacement for Judas Iscariot, the lots were divided amongst Mathias and a few others. No one was disappointed when Mathias was chosen.

"I'm going away soon." The words fell like a heavy blanket from Jesus's lips.

The disciples had gathered in the upstairs room of the Top Shelf Bakery, which was now their favorite place to meet together.

"Go? Where?" Mathias was the first to ask the question.

"Back to my Father's house," replied Jesus. "You will all stay here and be my witnesses, but it won't be easy."

Jesus was somber. "I will send you a helper, and I want you to wait here until he comes to you. He will empower you with my strength, and you will establish my kingdom everywhere. In the meantime, I will be preparing a place for you so that you can be where I am forever."

With that, Jesus went around the table and bathed each man's feet. As He washed them, He spoke to each one personally. With some, He shared a funny memory. With others, He prophesied about their future. When He came to Rufus, He paused for a moment. Then, looking into his eyes, Jesus said, "Young Rufus, you have seen much—and you must remember all that you have seen. You will share this truth with many until you have no more strength left and you are delivered over to your enemies. When that occurs, do not worry. I will be right there with you."

Jesus rose from the table and headed out toward the street. On the way past the kitchen, He stopped and embraced Simon.

"Thank you, friend," Jesus said to him.

Simon's eyes filled with tears as he held on to Jesus.

"Jesus, I believe," Simon managed to say.

"Yes, I know," came the reply. "I know…"

The group departed, single file out the front door. They were walking in the general direction of the Mount of Olives, though it seemed Jesus wanted to take some detours and walk the streets of Jerusalem. He seemed wistful and contemplative. As they approached the Mount of Olives, Jesus stopped suddenly. The air began to buzz, and everything seemed to be moving in slow motion. The sky became thick with angels as heavenly beings ascended and descended around the amazed onlookers. At that instant, Jesus began to rise, swept upward by angel wings until he disappeared from sight. He was gone. The men stood in the middle of the road, craning their necks and staring into the blue sky. After a few minutes, two men approached and stood with them. Looking up into the bright sun, one asked, "What are you looking at?"

"Jesus" they answered in unison.

"He will be back," said the other. "Just like He left, He will return in the clouds."

The disciples turned to ask him how he knew such a thing, but he was gone. There was no sign of either of them. Not in any direction.

***

Back in the upstairs room at Simon's bakery, the disciples talked long into the night. Rufus prepared hot coffee, remembering the concoction that he first tasted in Egypt at the shop in Cairo. Rufus recalled the Burmese man who brewed him the hot beverage made from roasted coffee beans. Rufus had made the special drink on several occasions since his Egyptian encounter, but he would be the first to say that the man from Burma made a tastier brew. Nonetheless, everyone seemed to enjoy Rufus's steaming mugs of dark coffee. The men and women who had followed Jesus began to gather in greater numbers in the upper room.

A week passed, then another. Business was thriving at the Top Shelf. Simon, still shaken by his experience at the hands of the Romans, poured what energy he had into his baking. He was becoming a wealthy man. He rented a large house in nearby Bethany. Gleaming walls of white stucco rose above his lush green lawn and gardens. The home featured a large veranda and four huge columns. The gardens were bright and colorful, and palms surrounded the wide porch. There, in that lovely setting, Simon and his son became close friends with Lazarus, whom Jesus raised from the dead. Lazarus, in turn, became a frequent guest at the bakery, where patrons considered him a local celebrity. They never grew weary of hearing the account of his resurrection, and for his part, Lazarus never tired of telling the story. Occasionally, members of the Sanhedrin would come into the establishment, where they would not hide their disgust for the goings-on inside. It was widely known that the Pharisees would like Lazarus dead. His popularity with the people made that threat seem impossible to carry out, however. As for Lazarus himself, he would laugh at the notion.

"I've been dead before, and Jesus gave me life," he was known to say. "I am unconcerned."

Little did the religious leaders know that at closing time, when the doors of Simon's bakery were locked, men and women who were awaiting Jesus's return would gather upstairs and pray. There was a sense of anticipation in their hearts. The pervasive thought was that Jesus had appeared to them in that upper room after His resurrection and he Had asked them not to go anywhere, so it seemed logical that He would return there and take them to the place Ge prepared for them. They did not know where Jesus had gone—but they did know it was *up* as that is how He had departed…in a cloud. They began to call themselves "sky watchers," for they were continuously looking upward for any sign of his return. There was a certain amount of fear within the sky watchers group. Joseph of Arimathea had heard there was to be a crackdown on those who asserted that Jesus of Nazareth was the Jewish Messiah. The Roman Empire was tolerant of existing religions, though it was considered a serious crime to establish a new ideology or framework of faith. Jews who were declaring that Jesus was the Christ, the fulfillment of the ancient prophecies, did so at certain risk. Jesus's resurrection from the tomb was proof positive for those who believed, yet rumors continually surfaced, challenging that he was merely hiding somewhere in Syria, awaiting the proper time to march upon Jerusalem.

The day of Pentecost arrived in Jerusalem as the Jewish nation celebrated the coming wheat harvest in the same manner as they had for centuries. Visitors from all over the known world filled the streets, commemorating the festival with family and friends. Stories of persecution, like the stoning of Stephen, were plentiful amongst those who gathered in the upper room of Simon's Top Shelf Bakery. The morning sun shone brightly out of doors, but the upstairs windows were covered and a sign on the doorway at the foot of the stairs read, "Storage—No

Admittance." More than once, Simon and Rufus, with some assistance from Mathias, carried a large crate up the stairway. No one in the bakery section would ever guess that the box carried a believer in hiding. Occasionally, a curious glance from a steely-eyed Pharisee would send a shudder through young Rufus, but suspicion, such as it was, never resulted in any investigation by the ever-present Roman guard.

Suddenly, as the morning sun climbed above the buildings, the darkened upper room became brighter than noonday. Flames of blue-green fire danced across the rafters and down the walls. They seemed to pick up speed and intensity by the moment, and from the flames came a beautiful harplike sound accompanied by trumpet blasts that rattled the eaves. Soon a roar like a mighty wind overcame all other sounds, and those in the room could not hear even the loudest voices as they shouted one to another.

"What is this?"

Their calls were swallowed by the rushing air. Eyes wide with both awe and delight, each person began to smile and then laugh as an incredible joy filled their hearts. They felt the way they had as children when their father returned from the sea or city. They began to dance and leap. They hugged each other and raised their hands to heaven. Then, incredibly, the flame split into many flames, and each one rested over the head of the Sky Watchers.

"This is him! It's Jesus!"

Rufus could not mistake the powerful presence of the crucified one. His heart was bursting with emotion. He felt like Jesus was in the room, but also in him.

A crowd was gathering in the street. The patrons that had been in the restaurant below had exited the bakery for fear the walls would collapse. The sound of hurricane force winds was so strong. Neighbors came out of their houses to see what had occurred. A cyclone? A fire blazing out of control? The upper room was quickly emptying. Not being able to contain themselves, the ecstatic group of believers spilled down the stairs. Standing on the top step of the entrance to Simon's shop, they all began to shout the good news that God was among his people. Every promise to the Jewish nation since the time of Abraham was now fulfilled in Jesus. This was a great day!

Jesus had been the "once-for-all slaughtered Lamb" that brought men to the Father. Incredibly, as their words rang out—they came forth in languages they did not know. Yet the crowd seemed to hang on every word with complete understanding.

Peter could not stop talking, and he launched into a speech that was as mighty as the wind that had blown through the upper room, minutes before. The fire was now within him, and many men and women believed his words about Jesus the Christ.

"We must baptize them all!" he stated.

Fittingly, it was Simon and his son, Rufus, who were the first to enter the waters of baptism.

"We must have baptized more than a thousand," said Peter, back inside after the crowd dispersed.

The disciples were exhausted and hungry. Simon served a meal of flatbread and bean curd which the men devoured.

"I think something has begun today," said Mathias. "I feel a new level of peace and power in my being. I cannot describe it, but I know it is from heaven."

Everyone agreed that there was something new within them. For the first time since Jesus had departed in the clouds, nearly two months prior, the disciples felt the presence of their friend and teacher.

A young, upstart Pharisee from the city of Tarsus was making a name for himself by running raiding parties into Syrian territory, in hopes of finding secretive cell groups of converted Jews and maybe even their elusive leader, Jesus of Nazareth. Saul had a group of well-armed followers who would join him as he made his way along the Damascus Road by the cover of night, often terrorizing certain homes along the route. Wherever followers of The Way, as these new believers called themselves, were exposed, Saul of Tarsus and his men would eliminate them.

I, Alexander, heard this account of the execution of the first martyr many years later.

The first few stones missed their mark. Despite the rage and anger the accusers felt, when it came to drawing first blood, it required more courage than they had yet summoned. Each hurled missile flew wide and high, past the kneeling man named Steven. He was praying; that was obvious. His face was serene, a sharp contrast to the menacing looks of his executioners.

Saul, the ringleader, was in charge of this deadly affair.

"Anybody going to hit the target? Do I have to do it myself?"

Up until this moment, Saul, a member of the Sanhedrin, had been holding the cloaks of the mob who stood around the doomed man at the top of the temple terrace. Saul had charged a hefty fee from each man who wanted a part in the execution. They had seemed eager enough to pay for the privilege, and yet now, they appeared hesitant. With a sigh, Saul tossed the coats aside and picked up a rock. Marching closer, he stood about fifteen feet from the condemned man. Without a second thought, Saul released a savage throw. It found its mark with a sickening thud. The force of the rock knocked Steven down into the dust. The blood flowed from the deep gash opened above his ear. Seeing that, the tidal wave of evil crested in the heart of each man. One by one, the rocks began to find their mark as the dying man became sport to the killers. Saul, back at his perch with the cloaks, fingered the coins in his pocket and smiled.

This was a strategic execution. Steven had been a leader in the renegade religious movement called The Way. Their growing numbers offended the keen Jewish dogma that Saul espoused. The Way claimed that Jesus of Nazareth was the fulfillment of the Scriptures, the prophesied Messiah. They claimed that after his crucifixion he had laid in a borrowed tomb for three days. The common punchline amongst his followers went something like this: "He only borrowed the grave because He wasn't going to need it for long!"

Saul bristled at the thought.

Looking at the corpse of the dead man lying where he fell in the bloody dust, he said, "You gonna rise up too? I doubt that." And with a chuckle, he mounted his horse and rode away.

He went straight to his favorite tavern, where the talk was plentiful and the drink flowed freely. Saul was a bit of a local celebrity in this kind of environment. The area Jews appreciated his efforts to quell the ranks of the upstart Sunday worshippers, even the Romans allowed him free rein in dealing with the Christ followers. The last thing governing Rome wanted was a religious firestorm, pitting passionate factions against each other. This kind of thing had occurred in the past, with deadly results. Zealots of the Jewish faith had attacked soldiers of the Roman army on numerous occasions. As far as Saul was concerned, Jesus of Nazareth was just another misguided enemy of Rome and the Jewish power structure. Rome and Israel would both like an end to the growing group of Christians, as they had become known. And Saul was their man to bring down the final curtain on the sect. No one was safe from his deadly pursuits—not if they believed that Jesus was indeed, the Messiah. Women, children, the elderly—all were fair game. Now Saul had some more momentum. The stoning of Steven had taken out a ringleader of the church, and surely, there would be those who were now frightened.

"We are driving them underground and then into oblivion," Saul announced to the group of men at the bar where he stood. "Just like their misguided Messiah, underground and soon to be forgotten."

Hearty laughter rose from the men and carried out the open windows and into the night.

"There is a growing number of the followers of The Way in Damascus," Saul read the report the next day with interest. He could not have guessed that divine help was on the way to assist and strengthen the persecuted followers of Jesus.

Simon Sings

Months passed. The Top Shelf was busy every day, which meant Simon and Rufus were busy as well. Mathias had departed for Antioch, where a growing number of believers were gathering. Being recognized for his international travel experience and exposure to a variety of cultures made the newest disciple a natural choice for leadership in the new fellowship, which they began to call "church." The members began using a new title as well. They chose the name "Christians," meaning "little Christs," a verbal tribute to the indwelling Christ spirit they had all known since the fiery baptism into joy they had all experienced in the upper room at Pentecost.

News from Cecile came unexpectedly and hard. A courier arrived one morning with a message from our home in Cyrene. I, the younger brother of Rufus, Alexander, had become deathly ill. I had developed a cough which became a fever. My mother and aunt stayed by my side, packing me in cool, wet blankets and trying desperately to coax me to drink the broth that they had prepared for me. Yet I was getting worse, not better. I drifted in and out of sleep, and my words became unintelligible. Cecile was afraid that I was dying. She had closed the bakery and summoned every doctor she could find.

"I've got to go to Cyrene," Simon announced, back in Jerusalem. "I will leave in the morning. I will hire a chariot and a team of horses. I can be in Cairo in a matter of days. From there, I will sail home to Cyrene."

Rufus was anxious at the thought of staying in Jerusalem without his father, but he was now nearly seventeen, and considered to be a grown man. He would take care of business during Simon's absence. Rufus recalled the day of the gladiator battle when Thomas of Thera was cut down with the mighty Egyptian fighter's weapon. That was the day his father had first entrusted him with the collection of money from the patrons of the original Top Shelf Bakery. He remembered how important it made him feel to assist his father and track the sales. Now, he felt that way again as he contemplated the plight of his brother.

"You can count on me to keep things in order here," Rufus remarked. "Don't worry."

That evening, Peter came by the shop to visit. It was good to see the former fisherman. He brought a warning, however. The persecution, affecting followers of The Way, had been formally stepped up by a legal document issued by the Jewish court of the Sanhedrin. The document outlawing the new sect had been posted at the temple and a written copy had been delivered to Saul of Tarsus, qualifying him to openly persecute and destroy the followers of The Way who would not renounce their faith in Jesus, "their pitiful and absent Messiah." Thus, the decree stated. Jerusalem was not a safe place to be known as a Christian.

"You must go to Antioch and be with your Uncle Mathias." Simon's words to Rufus were firm. "It's safer there."

Simon then explained to Peter that he was also departing in the morning, heading home to Cyrene. He informed him of the urgent message from Cecile.

"I once saw Jesus heal a centurion's servant, even though he was miles away from him at the time," said Peter. "Let us pray now in the name and authority of Christ for Alexander to be made well there where he lies in Cyrene."

The trio got down on their knees and called upon the resurrected Christ who ascended to heaven and then descended like a raging firestorm within them to bring miraculous healing to me, Alexander. They each lifted their voices in prayer, calling on the name of Jesus of Nazareth. As they finished, Rufus was sure he saw a lone figure disappear from the doorway. He ran to look outside, but whoever it was had vanished. Rufus shrugged his shoulders and returned inside.

"I've got an uneasy feeling that we were being observed," Rufus said to Peter. "Everyone knows we close at the supper hour, so I doubt it was a customer."

"That is not good," replied Peter. "Simon, you had better leave Jerusalem before dawn and, Rufus, I will get you to Antioch."

Rufus could see the concern on Peter's face. "When should I leave?" he asked.

"Tonight," said Peter.

Later that night, Rufus said a tearful goodbye to his father. The two held each other in a long embrace while Peter waited impatiently at the door.

"We have to go!" said the rough and ready "rock" as Jesus had once called him.

Rufus then climbed under some blankets on the back of a waiting farmer's wagon and the creaking wheels started to turn in the muddy ruts, beginning the ride that would take them north and then westward to Antioch. The driver was the disciple known as Philip, in heavy disguise. To the casual observer, the cart seemed to be nothing more than a farm transport making a delivery. Simon stood in the doorway of the bakery and watched until the cart could no longer be seen through the gloaming.

The cart's journey would bring them out of Jerusalem, and they would then join the King's Highway toward Syria. From there, they would reach the Via Maris, the roadway that would take them through to their destination, some three hundred miles away. As the donkeys pulled the wagon farther and farther from the city, Rufus sat up next to Philip. The hour was late, and the countryside sparsely settled. The road to Damascus had few travelers, despite the bright light of a full moon, that now rose above the distant mountains.

"We have good weather for travel," said the soft-spoken disciple.

Rufus shivered despite the warmth of the night air.

***

Back in the city, Simon hung a sign in the window of his establishment. It simply read, "Closed until further notice." He washed a few dishes and put away pans and utensils. Finally, he swept the floor and closed the curtains. He stood in the doorway and looked back at his bakery. It had been the success he had hoped for back in Cyrene, and yet he felt strangely detached from the enterprise. He was a wealthy man now, but it seemed unimportant to him. He felt an uneasiness that he could not explain. He could tell the hour was late, and he was not anxious to travel home to Bethany. Going back into the kitchen, he took some blankets and made a bed for himself on the floor. He awoke before first light and washed his face in the basin on the counter. Grabbing his cloak and some provisions, he turned the key in the lock on the front door and headed for the livery where he would hire an enclosed chariot and a team of stallions. As he walked the few blocks to the stables, he felt a strange sensation, as if he were being followed.

"Nonsense," he muttered to himself. "You're imagining things."

He arrived at the gate of the municipal corral, and within minutes, he had selected some fine horses and a lightweight four-wheel chariot with room in the rear for his luggage and a captain's chair in the front where he could sit during the long journey. He had just finished securing the gear when a voice behind him said, "Where do you think you're going?"

Simon straightened up and looked over his shoulder. Four men were standing in the dawn's early light. When he turned back, there were four more that had moved in front, blocking his way. One of them grabbed the bridles of the horses and held on.

"What do you want with me?" Simon asked, feeling the fear rise in his throat.

It seemed obvious to him that these men meant to do him harm. He tried to run, pushing the line of ruffians but not breaking through. They instead shoved him to the ground. He landed in a heap in the dust but quickly scrambled to his feet.

"Where is your son?" one of the men demanded.

"My son lies sick in his home in Cyrene." Simon did not lie although he knew it was Rufus they were looking for. "I am headed for Cyrene now to go to him." Simon's voice quavered.

"Do you deny that you are a follower of Jesus of Nazareth?" One of the men stepped forward with the question.

"Why do you ask?"

"Because your very life depends upon your answer."

The man was so close now to Simon that the frightened baker could feel the stranger's hot breath on his face.

"Who are you to threaten me so?" Simon felt a strange courage rising within him as he shot back his own question.

"I am Saul from Tarsus, and I have authority to eliminate the followers of the dead self-proclaimed Messiah. Now, answer! Do you follow Jesus of Nazareth?

Simon did not answer. Instead, he looked skyward and lifted his hands in prayer. The eight men picked up rocks from the stony ground and stood, ready to throw them upon command. Saul shook his fist in Simon's face.

"Where is your son? Where is Rufus?" he demanded.

Simon looked directly at Saul and said evenly, "You will one day meet my son, Rufus. When you do, be sure to tell him that I will wait for him in the land of the living, in the kingdom of Jesus, the Christ."

Saul snapped back, "A confession if I ever heard one!"

With that they tied Simon's hands and feet and pulled the rope tightly. The first few rocks sailed high, but the men soon found their mark. Simon did not cry out. He closed his eyes and began to sing. The words came from somewhere deep within his soul. The men who were stoning him were certain that they could hear two voices, one from Simon and one from the sky above.

He chose his servant
and took him from the flocks and fields;
from tending the sheep, he brought him
to be the shepherd of his people,
of Israel his inheritance...

Just as a large stone crushed his skull, Simon spoke his final words. They were whispered softly but clearly, "Jesus. I believe."

At that same moment, hundreds of miles away, I, Alexander, a certain young man of Cyrene sat up in my sickbed. I cannot explain what happened, but I was well again. I cheerily bounded into the kitchen and announced to my astonished mother, "I am hungry!"

"And you are well again, my child." Mother sobbed, as I fell into her arms.

ANTIOCH

Rufus
"Rufus and Simon are gone."

Saul and his men dug a shallow grave outside the city wall. If anyone saw them dump Simon's lifeless body in the ground, they were unaware of it. They covered the corpse with loose soil and placed rocks over the site.

"The jackals may dig him up," said one of Saul's men.

"Or Jesus's followers may try to stage another resurrection," said another.

"If either man or beast try unearthing him, they can have him," Saul countered.

With that, the men brushed the dirt from their clothes and went back into the city.

"I'm buying breakfast," said Saul. "But it won't be at the Top Shelf Bakery. I have a feeling they will be closed for a long time."

A ripple of laughter filtered through the group as they made their way down an alley which opened up to the main street, where the eating establishments were just opening for the day. The smell of garlic hung heavy in the air, and the men found themselves suddenly hungry. They ducked into a small café and ordered enough food for twice as many men. Saul was in good spirits. He toasted the men around the table and thanked them for their service to Israel.

***

Later that morning, some two miles from Jerusalem, Lazarus knocked on the door of Simon's home. He was anxious to see his friend and to hear any news from Cecile regarding Alexander's condition. No one answered his knock. He called to Simon, but still, there was no response. Thinking his friend had gone into Jerusalem early to open the shop, Lazarus jogged into the city. There he found the note on the bakery door stating the Top Shelf was closed until further notice.

Huh, thought Lazarus, *I wonder where he could be?*

"Lazarus!" It was Peter's familiar voice he heard. "Lazarus, come across the street. I will tell you what's going on."

Lazarus crossed the street and followed Peter to a small park. When he was certain they had not been followed, Peter turned to Lazarus and spoke in a hushed tone.

"Rufus and Simon are gone. The threat against them was growing, as it is for all of us. Simon has left for Cyrene to assist Cecile. Alexander, as you have heard, is gravely ill. He left very early this morning. Rufus, on the other hand, is en route to Antioch, where Mathias now lives. He departed last evening and is probably over the Syrian border by now. He is travelling on board a farmer's cart, and Philip is at the reins. If all goes well, they should reach Antioch sometime next week."

***

Indeed, all was going well on the King's Highway as the farming cart made its way north toward the intersection with the well-traveled Via Maris. Once on that route, they would have a straight shot to Antioch. They reached the turn in good time and headed onto the major westward thoroughfare. The towns of Kazir and Jezreel were welcome respites along their way. The pair enjoyed the hospitality of the townspeople in those locations. Descendants of the ancient Philistines, these local folks were known for being fantastic cooks. Rufus ate a tasty chicken dish on the night they stayed in Jezreel.

"It's the best meal I have ever had," he said to his travel partner, licking his fingers.

The next day, they passed the mammoth fort at Megiddo, once occupied by soldiers from Philistia, now home to a peace keeping force of international military men. It was an amazing sight to behold. Rufus felt a rush of excitement as they witnessed the changing of the guard on the columned portico. Pennants and banners floated in the breeze, colorful displays against the high blue sky. However, despite his excitement and the new experiences, a nagging dread was present in his chest—a feeling he could not shake. He thought he may be homesick or worried for his younger brother in Cyrene. He thought of his father and calculated in his mind where he may be on his journey home. Rufus supposed that Simon would have already reached Cairo and would soon sail for homeport. It had been more than a full year since Simon had seen Cecile, and Rufus was certain there would be a grand reunion upcoming. A wave of melancholy suddenly swept over Rufus. He missed his mother more than he had realized. The thought struck him that he may never see his parents again, and he choked back tears—or tried to. For a time, the travelers rode on in silence.

On the morning of the fifteenth day of travel, the city of Antioch was within sight. The donkeys seemed to sense the end of their long journey was nigh for they quickened their pace. A mountain pass opened before them, and they soon came to the busy banks of the Orontes River. There they got in line for the ferry that would bring them across the water to Antioch. Rufus gasped aloud when he saw the man operating the ferry. He stood nearly ten feet in height and was as muscular as he was tall. He was clad in a leopard skin tunic and his long, flowing beard was tied in braids. As the ferry docked and loaded its cargo each time, the giant would set on board huge barrels and boxes, transferring them from the loading area and then, using a system of pulleys, power the boat across the nearly mile wide river.

"A son of Anak," said Philip to a mesmerized Rufus. "Giants once ruled this land, but they are mostly gone now. Obviously, there are still some who remain. I have not seen one since I was a boy in Ashkelon."

"Are they friendly?" asked Rufus, a bit uneasy.

"I imagine so," replied Philip. "But he looks menacing, doesn't he?"

The cart reached the front of the line, and the men coaxed the donkeys onto the flat deck of the ship. Rufus kept as far from the immense giant as possible and breathed a deep sigh of relief when they ventured out on the open water. The lazy river was a full mile wide at the crossing point. The bustling dock on the Antioch side was full of sights and sounds that Rufus could only marvel at. The spoken languages were foreign to him as were the signs posted for visitors to follow. The two men finally found the customs desk.

"Point of origin," the agent said routinely. He seemed disinterested in the visitors.

"Jerusalem," said Philip and Rufus together.

The agent put down his scroll and looked at Rufus. His dark skin and soft brown curls did not originate in Israel.

Rufus, noting the curious glance of the customs official, added, "Well, I am originally from Cyrene, but I have lived in Jerusalem this past year and some months."

"That's more like it," said the man behind the desk. "Reason for visit?"

"Visiting family," replied Rufus.

Without any more questions, the agent put an official seal of wax on paperwork that gave the men permission to remain in Antioch indefinitely. He dismissed the duo with a wave of his hand.

"Now, to find your uncle," Philip said as he shook the reins, and the donkeys began pulling the cart up the hill, leading away from the waterfront.

The multicultural city opened wide before them. Like Cyrene, Antioch had both Grecian and Roman cultural defining points... established centuries before by General Seleucas, a close friend of Alexander the Great, the city still bore many Greek influences. Upon Alexander's death, his kingdom was divided amongst his military leaders. Seleucas it was fabled, let free an eagle that eventually came to rest along the Orontes River on the site where he established the city of Antioch. Two large statues in partial ruin testified to the culture of Greece having an historical hold on the city. The first statue dominated the market square. It was a partially clad woman of great beauty.

"She is Daphne, goddess of Greece, daughter of Artemis," Philip said.

He had been to Antioch once before and seemed unphased by the silent figure. Rufus could not help but blush, and he cast his eyes downward as they rode past the monument. The second statue was a tribute to Alexander and Seleucus forever carved in stone, victorious in their warrior's stance. The Greeks had yielded to Rome's power a century before, yet these ancient statues remained, a solemn reminder of the passing of time.

The men were unsure of where to look for Mathias. The city was large and well populated, and the pair had no address to search out. Suddenly, a brown blur jumped up into the cart and landed in Rufus's lap.

"Cico!" exclaimed the surprised but delighted Rufus.

Indeed, it was Uncle Mathias's companion and pet, Cico the monkey. The creature immediately started digging in Rufus's pockets in search of a snack.

"You remember me!"

Rufus was pleased to see the little monkey. He knew Mathias couldn't be far away. He gazed around the city square, and his eye caught the familiar figure of Mathias, standing on the edge of the crowd. He was looking right at Rufus, and when their eyes met, he let loose a laugh that could be heard by everyone in the marketplace. Approaching the cart, he pulled Rufus to the ground and wrapped him in a bear hug.

"I knew Cico would find you," chortled Uncle Mat. "We have come to the docks for three days in a row as we did not know exactly when you would arrive."

Cico chattered happily, and Rufus couldn't help laughing too. Mathias was all smiles, and he spoke in excited tones. Rufus embraced his uncle once more.

"How was your journey?" asked Mathias.

"Uneventful, truly," said Philip.

"Good. Now, follow me," said Mathias. "I am taking you to church."

Mathias walked at a brisk pace away from the square and headed down a side street. He stopped in front of a plain house of stone and brick. Rufus could see children playing in the backyard, with several adults leading them in a game of hoops. The game was one that Rufus knew well. He had played as a boy in Cyrene. The object was to throw a wooden hoop through the air and land it on a barrel some twenty-five yards away. The laughter of the children did Rufus's heart good. They seemed to have a freedom about them that touched his spirit.

"The first generation of Christ's kingdom," Mathias spoke. "These are Christian children, the sons and daughters of the first followers of Jesus."

"Christian?" Rufus asked. "I have not heard that name before."

"It simply means little Christ," answered his uncle. "We have called ourselves by that name for a few months now, and it seems to have caught on."

"I like the sound of it," said Philip.

"Indeed," said Mathias. "Come on in and meet your brothers and sisters. We are a growing family."

With that, the three entered the house. A curtain hung in the hallway, and candles were lit despite the daylight in the home. The walls were also draped with curtains, and rugs were covering the floor beneath their feet. To their left, a side room offered lounge chairs, and the travelers were urged to sit and rest. A young woman brought a bowl of warm water and silently took off their sandals and began washing their feet. Rufus could not help but notice her beauty. She kept her eyes from his, focusing on her task.

"Who is she?" asked Rufus after she had finished drying his feet and had left the room.

"That is Evangeline, daughter of Malchus." Mathias noted Rufus's interest in the girl. "Her father was a servant of the high priest in Jerusalem and was present at the arrest of our Lord in Gethsemane. Peter struck him with a sword and cut off his ear. Jesus healed him on the spot and called him by name. Malchus was one of our first converts to The Way. He and his family have been with us now in Antioch for many months, escaping persecution in Israel."

A booming voice came ringing out of the kitchen, calling, "Where are my guests?"

The voice belonged to a tall, husky man who burst into the room where Rufus and Philip sat.

"You must be Rufus of Cyrene!" he blurted. "Welcome! I have heard much about you. I am called Barnabas."

Turning to Philip, he added, "Welcome, friend. I am glad to see you again."

From that moment on, Barnabas took Rufus under his wing. He showed him around the house with glowing words about the many Christians who called this their home. Rufus guessed there must be close to thirty people living there. Upstairs there was a great room where the Christians met daily for prayer and worship. There was a large kitchen one floor below and a grand table where they all ate their meals. Everyone wore a smile as they bustled about, but none bigger than Barnabas. He was obviously the leader of the church. He had been sent to Antioch by the mother church in Jerusalem to encourage the growing number of believers in that city. Rufus could see why. He liked him immediately.

Philip and Rufus were shown their room. It was a tiny pantry converted to a sleeping area with two cots taking up most of the floor space.

"It is more comfortable than the cart we rode in to get here," Philip said dryly. "But not much!"

He laughed at his own joke. Rufus thought it would do just fine. His bed offered a view of the kitchen where Evangeline was hard at work preparing the next meal. Rufus had never seen anyone more beautiful.

That night, after a delicious supper, the household gathered upstairs in the worship room. Malchus opened the meeting with prayer, and then he and his daughter sang a worship song that was unfamiliar to Rufus.

How great is the mystery of our Christ.
He appeared in flesh, a man like us,
He was authenticated by the Spirit
Angels saw his victory
That is now preached among the nations.
In this world we believe
We will join him in his glorious kingdom.
Amen.

"I felt as though my heart left my chest and settled next to her," Rufus told Mathias after the service was over.

The two walked around the large yard in the soft moonlight.

"I think you are lovestruck my nephew." Uncle Mat chuckled. "Her father has told me that she was asking questions about you. So perhaps it is mutual."

That night, for Rufus, sleep was slow to come.

Reunion

The next morning, a messenger from the Cursus Publicus, the Roman mail system, knocked on the door. He was asking for Mathias. He carried a message from his sister, Cecile, in Cyrene. It read, "Alexander is well again, but I am concerned for Simon and Rufus. No contact from them. Please advise." Mathias quickly summoned Rufus to come to his room.

It was true, the illness that had racked my body and had me bedridden for weeks disappeared in a moment. Yet the concern that mother and I shared for Simon deeply affected every aspect of our lives together in Cyrene. Mother lost her interest in the bakery, and business slowed. I lost my belief in God, at least any sort of loving God who cared for our lives. I would not talk of religion with my mother. Instead I found some cohorts to befriend and found them more to my liking. These young men were atheists, believing in no higher power than their own consciences. I had a morbid thought that something drastic had occurred, and that my father, Simon, was dead. I wanted no part of a god who would take my father from me. So when some called my recovery "miraculous," I scoffed at the notion.

"When did your father leave Jerusalem for Cyrene?" Mathias was serious, and his words caused Rufus to take a deep breath.

"He left early in the morning on the same day I left, just hours after I departed. At least that was the plan," said Rufus uneasily. "Why? Is something wrong?"

"I'm not sure," replied Mathias. "I just received a message from your mother. She reports that Alexander is well, but she is concerned for you and your father. She does not know your whereabouts. I hope Simon got out of Jerusalem safely. The persecution of Christians is at a fever pitch. One of the deacons in the old city named Stephen was stoned to death by a zealous band of men led by Saul of Tarsus. They gave him no trial. There was no defense. His crime was to serve the poor and needy in Jesus's name. We just heard the news late last night. Some pilgrims travelled through Israel from Al Karak and saw the whole thing unfold. They brought word of their experience with them. They sailed here from Haifa and are going through to Rome. They say that Saul hopes to destroy all followers of Jesus, and he has the temple backing to do it."

"But my father has not been a believer for very long." Rufus felt queasy again, like he did on board the cart along the Via Maris.

"Let's assume nothing," said Uncle Mat. "Someone must know where he is."

***

At that very moment, hundreds of miles to the southeast, Saul of Tarsus, was on horseback, leading a band of men who were determined to blot out the followers of Christ. They were making their way north on the Damascus Road, headed for Syria. The words of a doomed man still haunted him.

"You will surely meet my son, Rufus one day."

He could not shake the image nor the sound of the man's voice.

"This could be our day to meet, Rufus. I will be ready if it is." Saul muttered the words under his breath. He looked down at his hands holding the reins of his mount. The now familiar bloodstains on the palms of his hands had appeared again. Shaken but determined, he rode on.

***

In Antioch, the days passed with no word from Simon. As the days turned to weeks, then months, the church members came to the conclusion that something terrible must have happened to the baker. Mathias sent a letter home to Cyrene, explaining their fears. He asked for Cecile to come to Antioch with me, Alexander, and meet

Rufus there. Cecile sent word back that she would close up the house and lease the Top Shelf Bakery to a local businessman, then sail across the Mediterranean to Antioch. If all went well, she would arrive in about one month. Rufus was worried about his father and excited to see his mother, but he had most of his attention on the daughter of Malchus. He spent a lot of time in the kitchen, helping out wherever he was needed. The women smiled secretively as they watched Rufus go to great lengths to be assigned duties that Evangeline shared. The friendship that was growing between the two was obvious to all.

One evening, at the dinner hour, Rufus saved a seat next to him, and when Evangeline brought the main dish from kitchen to table, she shyly bypassed her usual place to sit by Malchus and took the empty chair next to Rufus. Rufus beamed, and he was suddenly aware that everyone at the table was smiling at them. Old Barnabas got up from his place at the head of the table and put his arms around the embarrassed young people.

"You two have my blessing. Malchus, does your daughter have your permission to accept the courtship offerings of young Rufus?"

"If I say anything but yes, I may be disowned by my daughter." Malchus laughed.

Rufus was quite sure he had never been so happy. Uncle Mat wiped a tear from his face and stood to his feet.

"A toast, then," he said. "A toast to Rufus and Evangeline."

Everyone clapped and then prayers were offered up on the couple's behalf. They were young, but both were mature. With the widespread persecution of Christians, they understood their time together was likely to be short-lived. Antioch was safer for believers than Jerusalem, but not by much. Still, the merriment around the table continued past the dinner hour. Evangeline giggled as she playfully put her apron on Rufus.

"If you truly love me, you shall have to prove it by helping me clean the dishes," she said with a grin.

"Bring me every dish in the house!" he responded. "I shall gladly wash each one."

Meanwhile, the persecution of believers spread like wildfire under the direction of Saul, the zealot from Tarsus.

One morning, Barnabas stood up from the breakfast table.

"I have news from Jerusalem," he said, clearing his throat. "It seems we have a miracle conversion on our hands. I have it on good authority that Saul of Tarsus has been preaching salvation through Jesus of Nazareth. He has lost his position in the synagogue and is travelling about, testifying that he is now a Christian."

"A likely story," said Malchus. "I have known of Saul for many years, and he detests followers of The Way. He is an arrogant and violent man. I am sure that now, he is just trying to infiltrate the church and probably aims to draw believers out into the open so he can torture and kill them."

"That could well be the case," offered Barnabas. "But dear Ananias in Damascus has written a letter in Saul's defense saying that Jesus appeared to Saul and spoke to him personally. He has sent copies of the letter to James in Jerusalem and to Thomas in Samaria. I expect a copy to be coming here as well. Myself, I will leave for Damascus tomorrow so that I may hear him preach in the synagogues. I will know if we share the same Spirit or not."

Barnabas sat down again. A hush hung over the table as everyone considered the report.

"Oh, and one more thing," added Barnabas, "he has changed his name from Saul to Paul."

"I think it sounds like Jesus—to appear to the least likely convert and make him into a son of the kingdom," Rufus said thoughtfully. "The day my father carried the cross up Calvary's hill, Jesus was forgiving to those who pounded the spikes into His flesh. He told me that I would not understand what was happening at that crucial moment but that later I would comprehend it. I believe I am slowly understanding… It is all about God's unconditional love for every person, and no one is beyond reach."

Rufus then bowed his head and prayed aloud for Barnabas to have a safe journey to Syria and that the Spirit would give him wisdom and favor.

"Thank you, brother," said Barnabas.

The very next day, a runner came from the docks on the Orontes. He knocked loudly on the door of the house that Rufus and Philip now called home. The messenger handed a folded note to Clopas, who had answered the knock. Clopas was preparing to leave with Barnabas for Damascus. The two had prayerfully considered the travel plans, and both thought it would be safer to travel together. Barnabas, who was standing right behind Clopas, took the note and held it up to the light of the morning sun.

"It's a letter," he said, breaking the seal and removing the message from its envelope.

Turning to Rufus, he said, "I believe this is for you."

Rufus scanned the writing on the paper and then threw it up in the air. "She's here!" he exclaimed.

He could not contain his joy. Grabbing Evangeline by the hand, he started running for the waterfront. A large three-masted sailing vessel had docked at the international wharf and its passengers were disembarking as the couple approached.

"I am nervous to meet your mother, Rufus," Evangeline admitted.

"She will love you!" Rufus countered. "I know this is true."

Together, they studied the off-boarding throng, Rufus describing his mother and little brother to Evangeline, while she scanned the scene, looking for anyone who may fit the ongoing description.

"There," she pointed.

A young man and a middle-aged woman were making their way off the pier.

"That's too big a person to be Alexander," claimed Rufus.

However, the more he looked, the more he realized that it was me, for he could now see Mother by my side. She saw him at the same instant, and no words were spoken. None could be found to express the relief and happiness they felt as they ran into each other's embrace.

"My son, Rufus!" Cecile managed to say, after finally stepping back to take a good look at her boy—now a man.

"Mother!" chimed Rufus. "I am so glad you have come. Have you any news of Father?"

A cloud of heartache overcame them both at the mention of Simon.

"I was hoping that you had news, my son." His mother's eyes brimmed with tears.

"Not a word," said Rufus. "But I do have other news."

With that, he introduced his mother to the lovely Evangeline. "We are betrothed to one another," Rufus said with a huge smile.

"It appears I have a story to hear," said Cecile.

"And you shall hear it!" crowed Rufus. "Alexander!" he went on. "You are taller than I am."

Rufus stood on his tiptoes next to me, and said, "I barely recognized you."

The merry group gathered their travel bags and began the walk toward the house. All the way there, we spoke of home in Cyrene and the voyage to Antioch. As they approached the dwelling, Mathias came running out of the main door and scooped up his sister in a great hug.

"Mathias, put me down," Cecile pleaded to no avail.

"Cecile, it is good to see you, my sister. Can this be Alexander?"

Before I could answer, I was overtaken with laughter as Cico jumped onto my shoulder and then my head. The little creature immediately began fishing through my pockets.

"It is you—only bigger!" said Mathias. "Cico remembers."

"Hello, Uncle Mat, and hello, Cico." It was good to see them.

Soon, we settled into the routine of the early church. It was only a matter of days before Mother came to believe the testimony of the family of God there in Antioch. Cecile saw the evidence of love, grace, and peace that marked the early Christians. Rufus explained how Jesus had transformed them by his sacrifice on the cross and resurrection three days later.

"And he left us his spirit to live within us—affecting all we say or do," he told his mother.

"Did your father believe this as well?" Cecile queried.

"He came to believe it, yes," Rufus replied, reflecting on the many months in the city of Jerusalem.

They had journeyed there from Cyrene in order to establish themselves as bakers, but somehow, after encountering Jesus, profit and sales were not as important. They had lost their lives to the cause of the good news that God loves people but had discovered their new lives as children of the heavenly Father. Now they were carriers of that incredible love.

Bad news seemed distant for a time. The weeks went by with an uneventful evenness. The pressure of persecution was widespread in Jerusalem. However, the believers in Antioch enjoyed relative freedom from naysayers and religious zealots' intent on destroying the new theology. Barnabas returned from Damascus with a report on the dramatic conversion of Saul, now called Paul. He had been preaching in the synagogues and public places. He had been sticking it to the religious power structure that he claimed made Christ inaccessible to most people, by demanding alms and religious taxes, along with impossible rules. Paul was a self-proclaimed "sinner," saved by grace. It seemed his intense pride was gone, and in its place was a genuine humility. Barnabas arranged a visit to the city of Jerusalem for the two of them. His stated goal was to convince the church fathers of Paul's genuine conversion. He set up meetings with Peter, James, and John as well as Matthew and a Gentile convert named Luke. The original disciples were most assuredly fearful of Paul and suspicious of his motives. He offered sincere apologies to the families of Christians whom he had terrorized or murdered. He called himself the chief of sinners and promised to try to win more converts to The Way than the number of Christians he had killed. Still, the men of Jerusalem were glad to bid Paul and Barnabas adieu. Paul then headed alone for the Arabian desert, where he would spend many months in seclusion in the study of the Scriptures. Barnabas headed home to Antioch.

Barnabas pulled Rufus away from the dinner table on the night of his return from Damascus. The meal was over, and everyone was busy with the evening chores. The two men went out into the yard and sat on the bench near the grove of sycamores. Barnabas was not his usual jovial self, and Rufus knew something was weighing on his mind.

"I have something to tell you, Rufus," Barnabas began.

"Yes?" Rufus felt his heart begin to pound in his chest.

"We now know what happened to your father," said Barnabas slowly. "It isn't good news."

"I have prepared myself for bad news for months now," replied Rufus bravely. "I am ready to hear whatever you have to say."

"While I was in Damascus, getting acquainted with brother Paul, I had the opportunity to have dinner with him. The Holy Spirit gave us understanding and wisdom, and a true relationship was born between the two of us. I told him he would benefit by coming here to Antioch. As I described our community here, I happened to mention your name. He became very serious and asked me direct questions about you. I could not believe he knew of you. However, he said he was destined to meet you."

"Meet me?" asked Rufus.

"Yes, and he grew very anxious at the thought. Then he asked if you knew of your father's death. I said we didn't know what became of Simon. 'He's dead,' Paul had then said. 'Are you certain?' I asked him. 'How do you know this?' 'Because I killed him,' Paul had stated matter-of-factly."

At this, Barnabas grew silent, and Rufus sat in complete shock. "Have you told my mother?" he finally managed.

"Not yet," said Barnabas.

"I will tell her," replied Rufus.

"When you do, be sure to tell her that Paul also told me where your father's body lay, and I sent word to Jerusalem. Some of the believers there retrieved Simon's remains and gave him a proper Christian burial. Nicodemus paid for a grave and a marker above it reads, "Simon of Cyrene. He carried our Savior's cross." Rufus could not hold the tears back any longer. He buried his face in Barnabas's chest and wept. Many minutes passed as the two men sat motionless. The moon rose and splashed light over the courtyard. As the night settled in around them, the silence was finally broken as Cecile leaned out the door and called them inside.

"You had better come out here, Mother." Rufus called. "I have something to tell you."

Days of worry and concern were replaced by days of sadness. No longer did they wonder as to Simon's whereabouts. Now, they knew, and they had a confession from the murderer. Anger mixed with the pain of loss. Rufus found solace in his kind and gracious

Evangeline. Cecile kept herself busy and spent much time with the women in the market or the kitchen. As for me, Alexander, I grew sullen and dark. I thought only of revenge for my father's death. Although I had just turned fifteen, I often stated a desire to be old enough to leave Antioch and the church.

"When I get older, I am out of here," I was known to say. I stopped attending services and instead hung out by the docks. Cecile was concerned about me, but she excused my behavior by saying, "You're just angry about losing your father. He is with Jesus now."

"Knowing Jesus was the thing that killed my father," I would retort. "A lot of good it did him."

FORGIVENESS

Cecile
"Cecile, known to all as Ma, took Paul on as her own project."

The wedding of Rufus and Evangeline was on a sunny summer day. The young couple stood on the beach near the mouth of the Orontes River where it joined the blue waters of the Mediterranean Sea. They exchanged their vows and kissed while Barnabas pronounced them to be "one in Christ Jesus." Cecile cried through the ceremony, as did her brother, Uncle Mathias.

"As far as I can determine, you are the first to be wed under the new covenant that Jesus established when he said, 'I will build my church.'" Barnabas had looked into the matter and could not find another wedding amongst the new Christians in any city where the gospel had spread. Although just sixteen years of age, the newlyweds were wise beyond their years, and they handled their relationship with God-given maturity. Meanwhile, Malchus was forming his own relationship with Cecile, who took comfort in the gentle ways of the man who was best known for losing an ear on the night of Jesus's arrest in Gethsemane. Peter had swung his sword wildly at the rushing mob from the temple and had opened a wound on the side of Malchus's head, leaving his ear hanging by the skin of his skull. Jesus had healed the wound with one touch, and Malchus had known at that moment, that Jesus was no ordinary man. He had become a follower of The Way and had moved to Antioch with his daughter, becoming some of the first believers to establish a foothold for the church in that region.

Evangeline's mother had passed away years before after giving birth to her only child. Malchus had raised his daughter alone, and now, for the first time in years, he found another woman that caught his attention. Before long, she had his devotion. Cecile and Malchus married exactly one month after their children were wed.

"Rufus, the time has come for me to bring brother Paul to Antioch." Barnabas was sitting at the table in the kitchen.

Rufus and Evangeline were preparing the evening meal. They had been married for almost six months and were expecting their first child.

"I plan to leave you in charge while I am gone. I have it on good authority that Paul is back in Tarsus. That's where I will look." Barnabas continued, "You know, we now have more Gentiles than Jews coming to faith these days, and Paul has a keen mind that can explain the scriptures to both Jew and Gentile alike. We need him here."

"I know he has proven himself to the apostles, but I still stumble over the fact that he took my father's life," said Rufus thoughtfully.

"No doubt," countered Barnabas.

"I have a few questions to ask him," Rufus spoke slowly and deliberately. "I want some details about my father's murder."

It was months after his announcement, stating that he intended to bring Paul to Antioch, that Barnabas and Paul got off a ferry boat docked across the river and hired an old man with a skiff to row them across to the city. Barnabas had found the former persecutor of the church, now considered a brilliant scholar and lecturer at his parents' home in Tarsus. It took some persuasion, but Paul eventually consented to the travel plan, and he had booked passage to Antioch. No small consideration in the departure of his home region was the fact that Paul's wife of ten years was irate over her husband's new faith. She would not let him come into their elaborate home in the city and openly condemned her husband in the marketplace and synagogue. She was unwilling to be reconciled and filed for divorce, saying, "This timid, sick minded shell of a man, I know not. He is not the man I married." Paul would later refer to his bitter marriage as a thorn in his flesh, an enemy message that constantly reminded him of his uninspired past life. He would say that he found humility was the natural outcome of such a painful partnership. He knew it would be a challenge beyond measure to save the world when he was at a loss as to how to gain his spouse's favor.

By any standard, it was a much different man that Rufus met on the banks of the Orontes River in Antioch than the fearless murderer he had imagined. Paul seemed awkward and unsure of himself as he stood on the wharf. He shook hands with the small greeting party but had to look away when Rufus said, "Welcome, brother Paul."

That evening, after dinner, Barnabas and Paul invited Rufus to join them out under the sycamores. The three men sat for a time watching the setting sun disappear over the distant mountains.

Paul finally spoke, "I have a message for you, Rufus. It comes from your father."

Rufus swallowed hard and answered, "Yes, Paul?"

"Barnabas has told me that you know I was responsible for his death. I want you to know that he perished nobly and bravely."

Tears coursed down Rufus's face.

"Just before he died, I asked him where you were. I intended to kill you both that night. We knew you hid believers in your bakery. Your father said that I would meet you one day, and that when I did, he asked me to tell you that he would be waiting to see you in the land of the living. Then he sang until the rocks snuffed out his voice."

"He saw Jesus, I know it," Rufus cried. "Jesus sang to my father as they carried the cross up Golgotha's hill. My father never forgot that. Do you recall the words he sang on the night he died?"

"I recognized them as a psalm of David," Paul said, lost in thought. "I heard them first in rabbinical school, many years ago."

With that, the former pharisee lifted his voice and, through his tears, sang,

He chose his servant
and took him from the flocks and fields;
from tending the sheep, he brought him
to be the shepherd of his people,
of Israel his inheritance...

"Yes, that is it." Rufus could not suppress a genuine smile. "Jesus sang that to my father at his death, I know it. Paul, I thought I had some hard questions to ask you, but after what you just told me, I have nothing but praise for Christ and forgiveness for you," he said.

"I must tell you, Rufus, it was as if we heard two voices singing that night," Paul remembered. "The harmony came from the sky above."

The men sat motionless in awed silence. Who could explain the bond of peace that now settled over the men? Men who just months ago were at incredible odds, one a murderer of another's father, separated by race, religion, and creed—now fellowshipping together as brothers.

Rufus eventually spoke, "This is the model of Christ's church on earth as it is in heaven. What a message we carry."

Paul added, "I believe I am called to share it with distant nations, Jew and Gentile alike."

Paul then listened as Barnabas and Rufus offered their agreement to his proposed mission.

"A message of such forgiveness and love could turn the world upside down," Rufus stated.

"That's the plan," said Paul.

In the weeks that followed, Paul often went down to the marketplace and testified about his encounter with the risen Christ. Many gathered to hear him speak. In those days, dozens of new believers joined the band of Christians, and these once small worship services now overflowed with converts who gathered in praise of Jesus. As the church grew, Barnabas and Paul became restless, however, and often unrolled a map on the great table after supper and circled regions where the Gospel of Christ was yet to be heard.

One morning, during worship, the room was crowded to overflowing as it often was. Paul was preaching about the truth of the gospel when the Holy Spirit fell on the church, driving everyone to their knees in reverence. The glory of God filled the room. Rufus, filled with the Spirit, stood to his feet and spoke words that changed the course of history.

He said, "God is setting aside Paul and Barnabas to travel to the ends of the earth in order to tell the world of the forgiveness found only in Jesus. We are to commission them for this duty. We are to support them in this endeavor. And we are to bathe them in prayer, asking God to give them boldness and courage."

With great enthusiasm, the church laid hands on Paul and Barnabas and began to map out a route that would carry them to Phrygia, Cypress, Iconium, and other cities where no churches had yet been formed. Cecile began a provision drive to stock up the two soon-to-be missionaries with clothing and cash. She did not consider Paul to be in good health, so she fed him a lot of hot soups and goat curds mixed with spices.

"I reckon that is how she works out her forgiveness for his murder of Simon," Barnabas would muse.

Her life full of good things, Cecile often said, "Christ loved us enough to go to the cross for our salvation, while we were still his enemies. What excuse would I have to offer if I treated my brother Paul with any less kindness?"

Another important person took up Cecile's attention during this time. Evangeline gave birth to a beautiful baby girl one warm spring evening. The windows of the house were open, and Rufus paced back and forth under the sycamore trees until he heard the cry of a newborn from the upstairs bedroom. He entered the room where Evangeline held a tiny but healthy little girl.

"Her name is to be Simone, in honor of your father," whispered Evangeline to Rufus.

Cecile was beaming. From that moment on, Cecile enjoyed a special bond with her infant granddaughter.

The friendship that grew between the family of Rufus and the missionary-minded Paul was truly remarkable. He enjoyed many meals in the home of Cecile and Malchus. Cecile loved to "mother" the former Pharisee. She would send him out the door each morning with a neatly packed lunch, urging him to take the time to stop and eat. No matter what she said, however, Paul would often get so caught up in a sermon or an argument, that he didn't take the time to enjoy the food. Most days, he gave his homecooked meal to a homeless beggar on the street.

The Roman Empire was open to a variety of religions, as long as they did not instigate rebellion against Caesar's government. The church in Antioch and Jerusalem was still officially seen as a splinter group of Judaism and thus tolerated to some degree. There were constant outbreaks of violence and many arrests of what was now called followers of The Way. However, these were largely localized and led by zealous vigilante mobs. The real trouble began when Rome issued a tax on the Jews. The Jews readily paid the tax and were left alone. Yet the church of The Way refused to pay the tax, thus breaking the perceived bond between Jew and Christian. Christians were out from under cover, being viewed by the government as a separate entity.

Rome decided to check on their allegiance to Caesar. Each emperor on the Roman throne took the title of Caesar and was considered to be deity by the general populace. Any citizen who would not testify that Caesar was god was faced with immediate deportation or, worse, execution. Christians were given one year to establish their allegiance to the Roman emperor. Most chose to face arrest and the likelihood of execution. The carrying out of these death sentences was swift and sudden, rarely would there be a trial of any sort. Captured Christians would be forced to admit their loyalty was to Caesar first. Naturally, most were reluctant to assert any such thing, despite the threats that were levied against them. Reports of stoning and burnings at the stake were passed on quickly from house-to-house and church-to-church. The empire was growing less and less tolerant of the followers of Jesus. But the church was growing despite the persecution.

In Antioch, the winds were shifting too. One night, a follower of The Way was kicked and beaten after closing up his garment shop. A group of young men attacked him and hurt him severely. The local thugs were led by one called Alexander. Rufus knew all too well who Alexander was, and it broke his heart. He pleaded with me to forsake the ways of enmity toward the church, but his words did not touch my heart. With a friend named Demetrius, I would often be seen at public places where Paul was preaching, shouting obscenities, and making lewd gestures.

"Pray for his soul," Paul told the worried family. "He has departed from the faith."

Days flew by. Rufus and Paul, along with Barnabas and Mathias, were busy making an itinerary for the upcoming missionary journey. It was to be a dangerous trip. There were enemies of the gospel message, and there were travel related dangers as well. Weather, difficult terrain, marauding bands of pirates all loomed ahead of the men who set a date in the early spring to embark on the journey.

As the time for their departure drew closer, a prophet by the name of Agabus came to Antioch. The church was growing as many Gentiles were believing in Christ as Savior and were being added to the fellowship. Agabus was received with honor and was taken in by Rufus and Cecile, along with Evangeline and her father Malchus. On the second evening of his stay, he asked his hosts to gather the leadership together for he had a message to impart to the church. So Barnabas and Paul joined them as well as Philip and Ampliatus from Cypress, a believer of great faith who had become a close friend of Paul's. Agabus stood in their midst and prophesied a word from the Lord.

"A severe famine is coming to the nation of Israel," he began. "It will be long lasting, and many will suffer, especially in Judea. The Lord has asked of you to ease the suffering of your brothers and sisters. Paul and Barnabas are to begin their journey by travelling to Jerusalem with an offering from the believers there. Give generously, for the need will be great." The gathering promised to do their best to support the coming need.

The next morning, Rufus went house to house knocking on the doors of all the Christians in the city. He told of the prophecy of Agabus and was received warmly. The outpouring was more than generous. Paul and Barnabas would deliver a small fortune to the believers in Judea, enough to stock up on supplies and to survive the coming lack.

Paul and Barnabas departed from Antioch on a warm spring morning. They caught a ferry that would take them to the mouth of the Orontes River, where it flowed into the Mediterranean Sea. From that busy seaport, they headed for Israel where they would deliver the money and stay for a short time with the believers there. But all was not well in Israel. Word travelled quickly that James, the half-brother of Jesus had been executed in Jerusalem. He had died a martyr's death by order of King Herod Agrippa. The egotistical emperor asserted that he, the king, was directly descended from the gods and his incredible speeches did little to dissuade the populace that this was, indeed, the case. He had a rare gift for oratory, and he was often heard to say, "My words will be remembered long after the Nazarene carpenter's sayings will be forgotten." By snuffing out the lives of the leaders of the Christian sect, he hoped to rid the nation of its influence. The entire church at Jerusalem was running scared.

About a week after the news of James's death, a welcomed visitor arrived at Antioch.

"Peter!" yelled Rufus as he saw his friend at the front door.

"Come in, come in! We had no idea you were coming!" said Mathias excitedly.

He was clearly glad to see the former fisherman. They ushered Peter into the kitchen.

"You must be hungry from your travels," Rufus said. "Evangeline, would you put together a meal for our brother?"

"I could eat a little something." Peter laughed.

Soon a group had gathered around the table as Peter explained, between bites, the goings-on in Jerusalem.

They all listened in amazement as Peter described how Herod had arrested him and had planned to execute him the next day. He described how an angel woke him.

"It was quite a punch to the ribs he gave me!" Peter rubbed his side as he spoke. "But then I am a sound sleeper." He told of walking past the guards, following his heavenly visitor. "All the while, I am thinking that I am having a dream." He went on. "But it was real. I followed the angel until we got to Mark's house. I knocked on the door and stood outside in the pouring rain. Young Rhoda came to the door, and when she saw me, she ran back into the house. I figure she thought I was a ghost."

They all shared a laugh, picturing the soaking wet disciple knocking and knocking while the group inside was too busy praying for his release to answer the door.

"Did they eventually let you in?" asked Mathias.

"Yes, but then, I came straight here. Jerusalem is off-limits to this fisherman for a while."

About a week later, news of Herod's death reached Antioch. It was a ghastly report. Apparently, he had collapsed while delivering a long speech from the royal balcony of his elaborate palace. An unusual parasitic worm had somehow entered his body, reproduced, and then literally ate him from the inside out. He died in excruciating pain.

"The world is a better place without him in it," Peter was heard to say.

Young John Mark arrived in Antioch with Paul and Barnabas. He was from Jerusalem, the son of wealthy parents. His objective was to interview Peter and to write down the story of Jesus. The new believers were desperate for information regarding the life and ministry of Christ. Peter's stories, where he often appeared to be somewhat foolish, were in high demand. John Mark had set out to write an accurate account of Jesus's life, relying heavily upon the memories of Peter. Together, they spent many hours visiting with the new converts to the growing church, most of whom were Gentiles from Spain, Africa, and the Orient. The varied ethnicity of Antioch brought many religions together. Most were abandoned after witnessing the miracles that accompanied the evangelistic efforts of Peter and Paul. Sick were made well, blind received their sight, and lame people walked. Every day it seemed the church was hearing testimonies of healings and other miracles.

"It's really happening," Rufus said to Cecile, one evening as they strolled under the sycamores. "The message of Jesus is reaching the whole world."

ROME

Paul
"The message of Jesus is reaching the whole world."

In those days, a new emperor had just come to power in Rome, and he was no friend to the Christians. Tiberius Nero was a reclusive madman who trusted none and eradicated anyone he perceived as a threat to his shaky rule. He hated Christians and commissioned his army to arrest and kill all those who followed the new religion. Rufus was sure it was not good news when Mathias reported seeing two ships at Antioch's central wharf, both filled with Roman soldiers. Uncle Mat had counted more than two hundred fighting men, plus weapons and horses coming down the gangplank.

"I have a feeling that things are changing," Mathias told Rufus, "and not for the better."

That night, Lucius, who had come from Cyrene, stood up at evening prayers and prophesied a severe crackdown on Christians throughout the world.

"We are going to require a presence in Rome in order to stem the tide of Roman influence and persecution. We need to walk the streets of the most important city in the world and bear witness for Christ Jesus right under the royal nose of Nero." Lucius began to weep as he continued, "The ministry will be arduous, and the costs will be high. Rufus, you and Mathias knew the Lord in person while he walked among us. You carry his heart of compassion and forgiveness. You must go to Rome and plant a church that shall grow strong believers in the faith. It is for this purpose that our Lord called you, years ago when he walked the streets of Jerusalem. He will surely walk with you again on the famous roads of Rome. Fear not. He chose you for this work. May God go with you."

Rufus was humbled and honored by the prophetic words of Lucius. At once, things became clear in his mind. He thought back to the last supper in the upper room of the bakery, as Jesus told the disciples that his body would be bruised and broken, but that it would multiply as one disciple shared it with another. Now, the body of Christ was spreading across the world. He remembered his father, Simon aboard a sailing vessel in the great sea, showing him the curve of the earth on the distant horizon.

He recalled the words his father told him that day. "We cannot see what is ahead of us, my son. But as we get closer it will come into view. So it will be with your life—the future will become clear as it gets closer. Be patient, and things will come into focus."

Now, Rufus would journey beyond where his eyes could see—to an unknown future, beyond the curve of time.

The weeks that followed were filled with preparations and packing. Rufus organized a small team that would travel with him and his family to Rome. He selected Mark and Lucius as well as Tryphena and Tryphosa, twin sisters who were strong in the Lord. They would help Evangeline and her young daughter who was now almost a year old.

One bright morning, Rufus awoke to a familiar voice.

"Sleeping while you have guests?"

The booming sound sat him up straight.

"Barnabas!" exclaimed Rufus, rubbing the sleep from his eyes. "You have returned! Is Paul with you?"

"Yes, he is down in the kitchen. I am afraid he cannot climb the stairs. He was nearly taken from us in Lystra. Jewish zealots followed us from here in Antioch and said many awful things about our church. They lied and called us a cannibal religion who eat flesh. They riled up the Jews in Lystra, and they organized a mob and dragged us outside the city gates. They stoned and nearly killed Paul there. He is still recovering."

Rufus was out of bed in a flash.

"You said these Jews were from here in Antioch?" Rufus asked as they quickly bounded down the stairs.

"I recognized a few of them," said Barnabas over his shoulder.

Together, they hurried to the kitchen. Rufus was not prepared for what he saw. Paul was seated by the fireplace, but Rufus had to look twice to make certain it was indeed him. He had yellowing bruises all over his head and neck. He was missing his front teeth. He had one arm in a sling, and he leaned upon a cane with the other. Most unsettling was the crevice in his skull, a dent that ran from the crown of his head to the bridge of his nose. It had healed poorly, and the dried scabs that covered it were an indication that he must have bled profusely from that serious head wound.

"Paul, what did they do to you?" Rufus knelt by his chair as he asked the question.

"They threw rocks at me. Big ones!" Paul managed to chuckle. "It's a good thing I have a hard head! I have discovered that it is through many hardships that we enter the kingdom of God."

Paul embraced Rufus, while Cecile, who had been busy at the stove, brought food and set it before Paul.

"I tried to sing your father's song as I was being stoned." Paul wiped a tear away from his eyes, wincing with pain as he spoke. With his voice cracked with emotion, Paul managed a line from the Psalm.

...from tending the sheep, he brought him
to be the shepherd of his people...

"It was the Lord's song," Rufus said into the silence that followed.

Witnessing the compassion that Cecile and Rufus displayed for Paul, Barnabas began to say, "How amazing the grace of God that brought bitter enemies into a loving family. The former pharisee named Saul is now the missionary, Paul. Together with the loved ones of the very man he put to death, he just sang the song of Jesus whom he persecuted."

"Only in Christ can something like this be so," said Cecile, giving Paul a kiss on his forehead.

The apostle blushed and called it a "holy kiss," much to everyone's amusement.

***

One rainy morning, Evangeline came running down the stairs and rushed into the kitchen.

"Where is Paul?" she screamed, cradling baby Simone in her arms. "My baby is not breathing!"

Sure enough, when Paul was summoned, he found the infant to be a pale blue color, and there was no sign of life.

"Give her to me," ordered Paul. He gathered little Simone to his chest and prayed in a loud voice. "Simone, breathe! In the name of Jesus!" Instantly, the baby sneezed and began to cry. Paul handed her back to Evangeline, who was crying too hard to even speak. She hugged her child, and the old apostle and held on for many minutes.

"Thank you, Paul," she finally managed.

"Thank you, Jesus." Paul smiled.

"Let's go find your daddy," said Evangeline as she headed back upstairs.

Paul sat down at the kitchen table and took a deep breath. "Yes, thank you, Lord." He closed his eyes and leaned his chair back against the wall. Within minutes, he was dozing peacefully, and his snoring filled the kitchen.

More trouble arrived with the coming of spring. The Christians began meeting just outside the synagogue in Antioch. This aroused the ire of the Jewish population which had, up until then, considered the believers to be nothing more than a nuisance. But this was also something new. The persecution also came from within the church ranks. Some converted Jews had targeted Antioch and had arrived there from Judea with a new gospel. It was a throwback philosophy that insisted non-Jewish converts had to incorporate aspects of the Mosaic law if they wanted to join the ranks of the followers of Jesus. Paul and Barnabas boldly took on the proponents of this doctrine in sharp debate, which, despite their best efforts, seemed to be gaining momentum. It was a major dispute, and there appeared to be no workable solution to the issue. Paul announced his intentions of travelling to Jerusalem in order to bring the matter before the mother church there. Barnabas and Peter elected to travel with him. Rufus was also selected for the trip, as was Malchus, Mathias, and Mark.

"I will be gone only a few months," Rufus told Evangeline. "I feel it will be good to see Jerusalem once again before we move our family to Rome."

The second day at sea, there was a howling wind that battered the ship. The waves became rough and angry, and the captain ordered all on board to get below decks. Mark was seasick and miserable. The boat was tossed about and taking on water. One particular gust of hurricane-like force cracked the timber of the mainmast. The ship was blown severely off course, having let the sails down to keep the mast from cracking in two. When they finally came within sight of land, it was the coast of Pamphylia. Mark exited the boat hurriedly, and once securely on dry land, he hired a chariot and a driver to take him back to Antioch. Paul was not pleased with the young man, but Barnabas was more understanding.

"He was pale and sick!" Barnabas defended the decision that Mark had made.

"I don't care," Paul shot back. "You don't quit in the middle of a mission!"

After almost a week in dry dock, the mast was repaired, and the ship sailed again. In just a few days, the men were walking the streets of Jerusalem. Rufus led the group to the former Top Shelf Bakery only to find it empty and locked. He went around back to the alley stairway, overgrown with vines and missing a few steps. Much to his amazement, the door to the second floor was unlocked. The men all piled into the upper room, dusty and dark though it was, while Rufus and Peter recreated the memories of those incredible days of being with Jesus. The group listened in awe as Rufus told of the last supper, where everyone sat and how Judas had stormed out. Peter told of the arrest of Jesus in Gethsemane and then looked at Malchus as he described himself that fateful night, wielding a sword that nearly got Malchus in the neck.

"I can hear better with this ear that you cut than my other one, oddly enough," said Malchus with a grin. "No harm done."

That night, the travelers met with the church leadership in the home of Mary, the mother of Mark. They wasted no time but set about to discuss the topic of non-Jews coming to the faith. Rufus described the events and ministry among the Gentiles. He also reflected on how he stumbled under the weight of the rugged cross on the day of Christ's crucifixion.

He shared the words of Jesus on that day. "No one takes my life. I give it away willingly."

Everyone was quiet, alone with their thoughts when Rufus added, "Since that day, I have carried the weight of his love with me everywhere I go. No matter what their race or creed, everyone is welcomed to come to Jesus."

"You were displaying phenomenal courage by attempting to move that cross and carry it for Jesus," said Matthew.

"Any other person would do the same," answered Rufus.

"Don't be too sure about that," remarked Peter. "I denied even knowing him."

"And then all of us ran away," added Thomas.

A sharp knock upon the door was answered by Mary. Two men stepped into the hallway. Rufus heard his name mentioned by one of the lowered voices. Then, into the room stepped Nicodemus and Joseph of Arimathea. Rufus jumped to his feet and embraced the men.

"How good to see you, my friend," said Joseph.

"It is good to see you as well," replied an overjoyed Rufus.

"We heard you were in Jerusalem," said Joseph. "Is that my old friend, Mathias?"

"Friend, yes! Old, no!" Mathias chuckled as he shook hands with the two men. "Come in and join our discussion," Mathias warmly invited.

The talk went long into the night, but it was finally resolved when old Nicodemus spoke.

"The Master once said to me that God loved the whole world so much that he gave his son to be a once for all, sacrifice for sin." Then he added, "Whosoever believes that truth will live forever. Notice he said 'whoever' believes. I am certain that it extends to the Gentiles."

Out of respect for Nicodemus and the late hour, the men closed the discussion there.

The next day, Rufus was given a sealed letter to be delivered to the churches at Lystra, Derbe, and Antioch. It stated the news that Gentile believers were welcomed into the church and were under no compulsion to obey Jewish law. It was an historic decision, for in a sense, it meant that Jesus was not only the Jewish Messiah, but the Savior of the whole world.

***

Back at Antioch, the believers welcomed the men home from Jerusalem. They had been gone almost three months and were weather-beaten and exhausted. However, Paul and Barnabas wasted no time in getting to the synagogue and preaching to both Jew and Gentile alike. Meanwhile, the friends who were headed for Rome to establish the church there were preparing to sail in just a few months. News from the region of Rome that reached Antioch was not encouraging. Christians, few that they were, had been forced underground, literally. The extensive series of tunnels and caves under the regal city provided hiding places for the believers. Mile upon mile of subterranean caverns lay beneath the city and these became home to many families. The pressure to conform to the Roman emperor became severe, and lately the colosseum had become the place where Nero sent captured Christians to face wild lions. Crowds gathered to witness the savagery as hungry lions descended on the defenseless believers, tearing them to pieces and tossing their lifeless bodies into the air, as a cat might play with a mouse. Rufus and his family would enter the city posed as bakers who planned to open a shop.

"We are good at that!" exclaimed Cecile.

"Hopefully we are just as good at opening a church," said Rufus.

Saying goodbye to the church at Antioch was brutally difficult. To complicate matters, a rift had formed between Paul and Barnabas. They were planning a second missionary tour, and Barnabas thought Mark should be given another chance. He spoke at length with Rufus about it, stating that Mark could join the team headed for Rome at a later date. Both Rufus and Mark consented to the plan, but Paul was firm in his stance that Mark was a quitter and did not want to "babysit" him.

"Once you are a quitter, you will always have that as an option," Paul explained.

"Where is the grace you preach about?" Barnabas's voice carried through the house as he followed Paul down the hall. "Would you like people to say of you, once a murderer always a murderer? I don't think you would."

Paul stopped, turned, and stared at Barnabas. "That's a low blow," he finally said.

"I'm sorry Paul," said Barnabas. "I don't know where that came from."

"I think we should split up for a while," Paul offered.

"Perhaps that is best," came the reply from Barnabas.

Paul departed for Asia Minor, while Barnabas and Mark left for Cypress. Paul had selected a new missionary travel companion… Barsabbas also known as Silas. The two had met while Paul was in Jerusalem and had become friends. Like Paul, Silas had suffered the loss of his family when he had chosen to follow The Way. His wife and children considered him crazy and reckless for having sold many of his possessions and donating the proceeds to the church. Silas's family moved to Crete, and Silas went out alone on the missionary trail with Paul. It would be a tough stretch for John Mark as he labored with Barnabas. He knew that he was not as strong of heart as was Paul. The words Paul had spoken lingered in his mind as he considered the weak assessment of his character that Paul had labeled him with.

"A quitter," Mark would hear himself say in quiet moments along the journey. Despite having the unwavering support of Barnabas and Peter, he felt sadness in his heart. He was responsible for the breakup of the mission team that the Lord had established when the church of Antioch had commissioned Paul and Barnabas.

"Paul doesn't trust me," he told Rufus in a letter.

"No, he doesn't," replied his friend. "But I believe someday he will."

Mark was somewhat encouraged and set about readying to join the church plant team in Rome as soon as he returned home from the missionary road with Barnabas.

Tiberius Nero, the Roman emperor, was disturbed by the reports reaching his palace of a growing number of followers of the dead king, Jesus. In a sweeping move, he ordered all Jews out of Italy. He was certain this would solve many of the cultural problems that faced his regime. He believed Christians and Jews were one in the same, just different expressions of the same religion. Those who chose to stay in Rome risked death in the coliseum. The lions were kept lean and hungry for just such an occasion.

"We selected a rough time to move to Rome," Malchus said one night at dinner.

Mathias answered him, "We didn't choose the time. God did. We just need to trust and obey."

A solemn discussion followed long into the night. Each member of the team pledged their very lives for the cause of the good news of forgiveness of sins and eternal life in Christ.

"I think we are just about ready to go," Rufus announced. "And may God go with us."

Exactly one week later, the small group of believers boarded a ship bound for Italy and the famous city of Rome. They were excited and frightened by what lay before them. They knew this was the grand purpose of their very lives. Mystery and danger would be their welcome, but their faith in the resurrected Messiah drove them on. They felt like messengers sent from the victorious army, announcing to all who would listen that the battle had been won. As they walked up the wooden gangplank, Rufus heard someone call his name. He stopped to listen, his eyes searching the crowd. He heard his name once more above the din of the dockworkers.

It was I, Alexander, his younger brother who was calling. He located me at last and began pushing through the crowd at the dock. We met on the long wharf where the ship was readying to cast off.

"I am sorry, brother." I looked straight into Rufus's eyes as I spoke. "I have hurt you and the cause you maintain by my words and actions. I regret that now." I hung my head while tears ran down my face.

"Oh, brother!" Rufus said joyfully. "I forgive you and our Jesus forgives you. Have you decided to become a Christian?

I lifted my head and said, "If you will have me."

"All are welcome," Rufus shared. "Don't delay. Do as I say. Go to Ephesus and find Paul. He will instruct you, and there is a dynamic church in that city with a young pastor named Timothy, I believe. Get involved in the work there. I am going to Rome, but in a while, you should come and meet us there."

"I will then," I said.

The ship's captain called, "All aboard that are coming aboard!"

Rufus hugged me as I said, "I'm truly sorry," once again.

Rufus finally let go of the embrace and ran up the gangplank, now empty, and stood at the bow.

'Goodbye, Antioch," he said wistfully.

In his heart, he believed he would never see the fair city, nor I, his younger brother, again.

Apelles of Naples

Apelles
"The Prisoner"

The voyage across the Mediterranean was smooth-sailing. There was a brief stopover in Sicily, but the captain was anxious to keep to the schedule, and so the ship pulled out of the docks after only a day on the large island. They sailed through the Straits of Syracuse, across the deep western waters to Rome. The drydock was a bustle of activity. Fish hawkers and farmers advertised their wares at the top of their lungs. Pushcarts and carriages unloaded baggage and trade goods. Rufus took the lead and bypassed the busy customs desk, unnoticed.

"Why let them know we are here?" He shrugged.

The group followed unseen and once on the street they gathered in a small huddle.

"Where do we go?" asked Cecile.

No one knew the answer. They were very hungry; that much they knew for certain. Scanning the crowded street, they made their way to an intersection and walked uphill on a side street to a café with sidewalk seating. They ordered the house special of fried fish and salad greens and found that the generous serving was enough lunch for all. As they prepared to pay the bill, the owner of the establishment refused to take their money.

"Hold on to your cash," he said. "Jehovah has told me to assist you."

Stunned, the travelers asked as one, "Who are you? How did you hear from God? Can you help us?"

"I am Urbanus," the host went on. "I am a new follower of The Way. I had a dream last night that I welcomed some brothers and sisters to this city and that you came to spread the good news. I was told in my dream to help you."

The tired group felt a wave of joy break over them.

"I marvel at the goodness of our God," Mathias said.

Urbanus took them into a private dining area and brought out an abundance of fruit and cheese, along with some red wine that soothed their parched throats. He then spoke to them of the crackdown on Jews and Christians initiated by Nero. The ancient café that Urbanus operated was well-known as the third of three taverns that were well visited stops along the main road into Rome. The first of the three was an outpost stopover two miles outside the city to the north. The second was one mile closer and the third, which Urbanus operated, was within the city proper. Most never knew it was also situated over an entrance to the maze of caverns under the city. This particular access was originally an exit tunnel for the emperor in case he had to escape an enemy attack and get directly on board a ship to take him away to safety. Urbanus lifted a portion of the wooden floor and revealed stairs descending down into the darkness.

"I'm afraid this will have to be home for you for a while," he said, lighting torches along the wall. "You can knock on the floor doorway whenever it is quiet above. I will send food to you and drink each day. Once it is safe and the persecution of our brothers is ebbing, I will bring you out into the flow of society."

"We came as bakers," said Evangeline. "We know kitchens very well."

"That may come in handy." Urbanus sighed. "I have long considered featuring a bakery as an extension of my tavern. It just may be time to accomplish that."

"How is it that you are safe in the city?" Malchus asked Urbanus.

"I am a Greek," he replied. "The Romans think we Greeks are too intellectual for religion. No one would suspect that I am a disciple of the Jewish Messiah."

Rufus could wait no longer. He asked, "How did you hear the good news of Jesus? When did you accept it as truth?"

Urbanus smiled and said, "It's nothing fancy," he began. "I was visiting my family in Athens some time ago. My brother, Dionysius, who lives there, is an aristocrat and prides himself on his knowledge. One day, during my visit, he took me to the meeting of his group of philosophers. It was there at the Areopagus that a funny little man came forth to speak of the god he served. He was laughed at by most. They called him a blabbermouth, but I could tell he was sincere. He said that God was not far away, but that he wanted to reveal himself to men and women everywhere. He quoted our poets and referred to a little-known statue that stood in the city to an unknown God. As he spoke, I found myself believing his words. My brother did as well. We knew this was the truth we were seeking. But he made his point and abruptly left the council. We called for him to return the next day and we hoped he would. We had many questions to ask him. He made it seem as though reasoning alone was not the way to reach god. In fact, it is true that our minds cannot figure out the Almighty and his ways. But if he truly does love us, that makes it a different story. Instead of us finding him, he comes looking for us. I am certain that it was no accident that I happened to be in Athens at Mars Hill that day. I will always remember it."

"Did you get to hear him speak again?" Rufus asked.

"We hoped he would come back for more discussion," Urbanus continued. The next day, we waited but he never showed. We never saw him again. I don't even know his name."

"Was he kind of hunched with a large crevice in his head?" Mathias was grinning as he asked Urbanus the question.

"How… How did you know?" stammered the surprised Urbanus.

"It had to be Paul," the group said in unison, each one smiling ear to ear.

They explained the apostle Paul as best they could.

"He sort of defies description," said Rufus. "He used to be a zealous murderer of Christians, but now he is a driving force for the cause of Christ. He actually killed my father."

"And my husband," Cecile added. "He nearly destroyed our family, but now he is like family to us."

"He is an effective speaker, that is for certain," said Urbanus.

"The best," echoed the group of weary travelers who already were missing their family of Christians in Antioch. But Urbanus's pleasant welcome and warm ways made them content to be where they were. This was to be their new home.

Not all Jews and Christians had departed Italy under Nero's command. Over the next several days, Rufus met Ampliatus, a rotund fellow from Sicily who loved to laugh as much as he loved to eat. Owner of the first of the famed Three Taverns on the outskirts of Rome, he had come to know the truth from observing the changed life of his friend, Urbanus. Rufus and Cecile met Phoebe, a wealthy woman from Cenchreae, a seaside village just east of Corinth. She had served the local church there but now had relocated to Rome. Because of her financial position in the culture, Phoebe was above any suspicion from the authorities who looked to deport or destroy all who followed the Way. Rufus and Evangeline also visited the house church run by Priscilla and Aquila, two schoolteachers turned tent makers who had befriended Paul during one of his travels. He had spent time with them in Corinth. He taught them the Scriptures. He modeled Christian living with both attitude and actions, and the three became lifelong, loyal friends. Rufus was then introduced to

Stachys, the business partner of Urbanus. A daring seaman, Stachys sailed as far north as Britannia and south to the lands of Africa. There was also a gentleman named Aristobulus who had a large family. He was also from Athens, but he brought his children to Rome in order to be free of intellectualism, which he disdained. He was a poet and a musician, and he held the attention of the early church many a night with his golden voice and harp. The caverns below street level provided excellent acoustics for the harmonies that came up through the floorboards after the café closed at dinner time. No one ever suspected there were Christians hiding from Nero under the sidewalks of Rome's busy thoroughfares.

Rufus and Mathias spent many hours each day, exploring the labyrinth of tunnels under the city. One afternoon, they came upon a low-ceilinged dark passageway that was too narrow to go through, but they could clearly hear something coming from the hole that caused them to pause. Incredibly the sound that reached their ears was that of a man, praying and singing. The song that he sang was familiar to the two explorers, a hymn of praise to the risen Jesus.

If we suffer, we shall also reign with him.
If we believe not, He remains faithful
for he cannot deny his own...

Rufus and Mathias looked at each other and then joined in with the voices behind the wall. As soon as they began singing, the voices on the far side of the stone blockade ceased.

"Who's there?" inquired the voice that belonged to the singer.

Whoever it was, he could not be seen due to the stonewall that divided the tunnel into two sections. Only sound could pass through.

"We are fishers of men," said Rufus into the hole in the wall.

He used a term that Jesus used when calling the first disciples, knowing only a fellow Christian would understand the reference.

"Brothers!" came the excited reply. Mathias and Rufus heard shuffling, scraping, and the heavy clanking sound of chains.

"Welcome to Tullianum Prison," said the voice beyond the wall. Mathias and Rufus swallowed hard.

Apparently, they had stumbled upon a path that led up to the back wall of the dreaded dungeon. The man on the other side of the stonewall was wearing leg irons and shackles. The men could hear the rattle as the prisoner moved about.

"What's your name?" Rufus inquired.

"I am Apelles of Naples. I was arrested seven days ago for speaking publicly about our Lord."

"You have been chained in this place since then?" asked Mathias.

"No, I was in a cell under Nero's palace overlooking his courtyard when I was first detained. I was forced to watch three of my friends being burned on stakes to provide lighting for the emperor's entertainment. Then some guards came and threw me into this cell this morning. Tomorrow morning at daybreak, they will come for me and take me to the coliseum to face the lions."

"Is there any appeal to stop this?" Rufus asked. "Have you been given a fair trial by a court of law?"

Apelles answered after a pause, "I am afraid those days are gone. Nero has made his position clear…to clear his kingdom of Jesus and the Jews."

Mathias then spoke. "We are not prisoners in a cell but rather Christians in hiding in the caves and tunnels under the city. We came upon this passage and heard you singing through a crack in the wall. We knew you must be a Christian brother, but now we know we are one in Christ with you. What can be done? We have not the tools or the strength to move these massive stones in a day."

"I would be grateful for your company," said Apelles. "Nothing more is needed."

"Then we will return before long with some other believers, and we will keep you company through the night," stated Rufus.

With that, Rufus and his uncle made their way back to where the others were gathered.

When it was evening, they sent Tryphena and Tryphosa up through the floor of Urbanus's café to get some bread and wine.

"We will share the Lord's supper together with our imprisoned brother, Apelles," Mathias said solemnly.

"And we will pray with him," added Rufus.

"And sing!" chimed Aristobulus.

As night settled in, the Christians began the rugged trail that led to the narrow passageway and the outer wall of Tullianum. When they arrived, they listened carefully by the stone portal. The sound of snoring reached their ears.

"Apelles is asleep." Rufus smiled. "He has the peace of Christ within. Let's not disturb him just now."

The group of believers formed a tight circle and began to pray. They prayed for Apelles, and they prayed for themselves. Each understood that the fate of the sleeping prisoner could easily be their own. They took turns listening at the wall for any sound from Apelles. The gentle, rhythmic snoring was all they heard. Then, as the light began to crease the sky outside, they heard the sound of keys and a creaking door. A guard's voice was heard.

"Wake up, prisoner! This is all you will get for breakfast, some bread and water. I will return for you in one hour."

"God bless you, sir," they heard Apelles say.

When the guard had departed, the clanking of chains suggested the prisoner was moving about. "Are you there, my brothers?" It was Apelles.

"Brothers and sisters both!" stated Urbanus. "We have prayed for you all through the night."

"How can I thank you?" asked Apelles through his tears.

"We brought bread and wine to share the Lord's supper with you," Mathias reported.

"I am afraid bread and water will have to suffice for me," said the prisoner.

"I am certain that will be fine," said Rufus. "Let's begin."

The Christians gave thanks for the bread and broke it, receiving it with grateful hearts. Apelles did the same on his side of the dungeon wall. They sang praise to Jesus, and they prayed for strength and courage. As they prepared to pour the wine, they heard the sound of laughter coming from the cell of Apelles.

"It seems we have a small miracle, my friends," he said. "I tell you the truth… The water that was in my cup is gone, and in its place, my cup is now filled with sweet red wine. It smells and tastes like heaven."

Everyone praised God for this simple yet powerful display of his presence.

"Just like his first miracle!" said Rufus.

Together, they drank and thanked Jesus for his sacrifice.

"Hush, now," urged Apelles. "I hear them coming for me. Farewell, brothers and sisters. We will meet again."

As the guards took him away, Apelles sang until his voice was swallowed up by the stone and brick, and he could be heard no longer. No one said a word nor moved for quite some time. The only other sound they heard that morning was the distant roar of the coliseum crowd as the lions were let loose.

UNDER THE STREETS OF ROME

Jesus and Rufus
"Someday you will understand."

Urbanus successfully expanded his tavern to include bakery items. At the same time, Nero grew somewhat tired of chasing down Jews and Christians, and so he stopped offering large rewards to bounty hunters who roamed through Italy seeking enclaves of believers. Many times, these bounty hunters would pose as followers of the way and thereby gain access to the meetings and fellowship banquets the early church was known for. Since the official response from Nero was one of boredom and waning interest, local tribunals were established to pronounce judgment on those found to belong to the early church. These were one-stop rushes to judgment, run by power-hungry men who sought to rid the nation of Jews. Roman guards were paid under the table to take away the prisoners and bring them to Tullianum where their names would be placed on a list. That list contained the order of those destined for the lion's jaws. Depending on the lion's appetite, the coliseum crowd may see five, ten, or twenty Christians die together at each of the grizzly events. Some doomed prisoners tried to run but to no avail. The lions were incredibly quick and would always capture their prey. Other men and women would form a circle in the center of the arena and hold on to each other for as long as they could or until their arms were severed from their bodies. Some unfortunate victims watched in horror as a great cat would hunker down to gnaw on a bone that had been attached to their own physical frame only moments before.

Still the church at Rome grew. Despite persecution, the gospel message was making its way throughout the world. A doctor named Luke came from Jerusalem to Rome to interview members of the fledgling church there. His goal was to produce a written account of the life of Christ that the church could use as a trusted reference. He had traveled with Paul after meeting him in Lystra, acting as his personal physician. The pair had become good friends, and Luke was a welcome addition to the church in Rome.

***

John Mark also arrived in Italy the following summer, having completed his missionary journey with Barnabas. Since he could speak four languages, he stayed above the Roman prideful suspicions of being a lowly Christian. Mark could easily use Hebrew, Aramaic, Greek, or Latin, depending on the needs of his environment. He spent much of his time writing at the home of Priscilla and Aquila. They were often away as they loved to journey with Paul when they could, leaving their house in Rome to the care of John Mark. His writing took on an urgent tone when Peter was arrested in Asia Minor and sent in shackles to face Nero. On death row, he was often visited by Mark, and together they compiled an account of Jesus's life and ministry, beginning with his baptism by John and concluding with his ascension to heaven. The guards tolerated the visits as it was their conviction that everyone was deserving of a last will and testament. Most of the prison staff assumed Mark was legal counsel to Peter. Mark carried messages from Rufus and the other believers meant to encourage the old apostle. As the day of his death sentence drew near, Rufus and Mathias decided that they would risk arrest themselves by promising to be on hand to support Peter at his execution.

"He is to be crucified at dawn tomorrow," Mark reported to the group of believers one day in the dead of winter.

"We must be there for our friend," said Mathias somberly.

The next day at first light, Rufus and Uncle Mat went to Nero's gardens where Peter was delivered. His eyes searched the small crowd, and eventually, he found Rufus.

As they looked at one another through the tears in their eyes, Rufus mouthed the words, "Farewell, old friend."

Peter whispered back and said, "Remember the Savior..."

With that, they nailed him to the cross. Peter insisted that they place him head down, and they did so. Peter had always made it known during the times of persecution and punishment that if he were ever called upon to endure the ultimate sacrifice and give his life for the cause, he would not consider himself worthy to die in the same manner as Jesus had.

"Remember the Savior!" Rufus could not restrain his voice, and he shouted encouragement louder still. "Remember the Savior!" cried Rufus.

Just then, a voice behind him said, "Come with me."

The arrest of Rufus was routine for the guards that took him captive. He was taken without incident. His mouth was gagged so as to keep him from calling the name of Jesus while he was being led away. His hands were bound behind him, and he was surrounded by twelve armed soldiers. They led him to Tullianum dungeon and tossed him into a filthy cell. He was without a light, and thus, the cell was in pitch blackness. He could see nothing of his surroundings. Even after his eyes had sufficient time to adjust to the dark, he could still see nothing. He felt for the edges of his prison and found metal bars and stone along the four walls. It was not a large area of confinement. The ceiling was low, and several times, while adjusting to the low clearance, he scraped his head on the damp stones that formed the top of the cell. He was not the only occupant of the cell. He could hear his cellmates scurrying around the floor. How many rats inhabited the dungeon was anybody's guess. He cringed as the four-legged creatures ran over his bare feet. He put his back against the back wall and tried to get comfortable, only to have the vermin fall from above, landing on his head and shoulders.

"Your ancestors did not defeat Joseph when he was thrown into an Egyptian jail," Rufus spoke aloud to the creatures. "You will not discourage me now!"

Still a tear ran down his cheek and a cry caught in his throat, as he recalled the story of Joseph that his father had shared with him on a night so long ago when they traveled through the land of the pharaohs on their way to Jerusalem. It seemed like a lifetime ago. So much had occurred since then. He wept for his family, knowing he probably would not see them again. He shouted to the stone walls, hoping against hope that someone would be within earshot on the other side as they had been for Apelles months before. But there was no sound that came back to his ears from the darkness beyond.

There he sat there for months, surviving on bread and water. He paced. He sang. He prayed. He asked for a blanket as the cold weather was coming in, but he received no such comforts. The church prayed for his release, but no good news was forthcoming. Then one morning, Rufus heard the guards bringing in a new prisoner. For a moment, the shine of a Roman torch touched the walls of the dark dungeon. Rufus's eyes were nearly blinded. The cell where they locked him up was out of Rufus's sight, but the sound carried easily. The voice was one that Rufus knew well. It was none other than Paul.

Through tears of joy, Rufus called out, "Are there any followers of Christ in here?"

Paul answered quickly, "I am one!"

"Paul, it is I, Rufus," he shouted. "I heard your voice, and it sounded nothing less than angelic."

"Rufus, brother! I have been longing to see you. How wonderful it is to be with you again."

"I like the company but not the accommodations," said Rufus.

The next three days were some of the most wonderful that Rufus could have ever imagined. Paul gave Rufus a complete rundown of the advance of the gospel into Gentile nations. He described the scene at Ephesus and the riot in that city that nearly took his life. He told of Philippi and the earthquake that shook apart a prison. He shared the story of being shipwrecked on the isle of Malta. Paul had Rufus mesmerized as he shared how he testified before Felix and King Agrippa and how the King himself was almost persuaded to believe the gospel message. He also talked about the extensive letter he had written to the church in Rome.

"It's a thorough document," said Paul. "It will serve as a foundation for the church for years to come. I entrusted the letter to Sister Phoebe, and she will keep it safe until it is delivered to Mark. I sent other letters to Galatia and Corinth. Everywhere the gospel is changing lives!" Paul reported.

He and Rufus praised God together, then prayed for the courage to face what awaited them at the hands of Nero.

The following morning, the sound of a key in a lock caused the two men to fall silent. Two guards appeared outside the cell of Rufus.

"It's time," said one of the guards. "The lions are hungry."

Rufus felt his knees buckle for a moment, but he gathered himself and stood straight.

"I am ready," he said clearly. "First though, let me say goodbye to my friend."

"Make it fast," said the Roman soldier.

As Rufus walked the short distance to Paul's cell, he thought of Evangeline and Simone. He considered his mother and Malchus and Uncle Mat. But most of all, he thought of Jesus—the author and finisher of his faith.

When he rounded the corner, he came face-to-face with the man who had killed his father so long ago. Now he had nothing but love for the little man with a dent in his head and bruises all over his body. He was missing most of his teeth, but his smile was genuine.

Paul said, "I need you to know that the forgiveness that you have shown me has allowed me to fully comprehend the forgiveness of Christ. It has fueled the message of salvation that I preach. It has moved my quill in letters that I have written. You have embodied the grace of our Lord and it profoundly affected me. I would not have dared to preach the forgiveness of God for sinners like me if I had not seen it modeled in you. Christ called you to be his own, and it was specifically for my sake. He allowed you to touch the cross he died upon, and although you were young at the time, he knew you would carry his cross for all of your days. Today you will exchange it for a crown."

"I have missed my father and my friend, Jesus. I long to see them both again," said Rufus through his tears.

"Yes, Simon said he would see you in the land of the living," said Paul. "You must go, but I will follow you in a little while."

As the guards led him away, Rufus heard Paul's cracked voice call, "Rufus of Cyrene and Antioch, Rome and the eternal Kingdom of our Christ. I have seen Jesus in you."

Then the old apostle began to sing.

He built his sanctuary
like the heights on Mt. Zion
like the earth that he established forever.
He chose his servant
and took him from the flocks and fields;
from tending the sheep, he brought him
to be the shepherd of his people,
of Israel his inheritance.
And David shepherded them
with integrity of heart;
with skillful hands he led them.

As he entered the coliseum, the song remained in his ears, but no longer was it the voice of Paul. It was his father singing to him.

Rufus felt as light as air. He was a boy again for a moment, back in the arena of Cyrene. Thomas of Thera was there. And Peter and James and Judas. Evangeline and Simone stood with Mathias. His mother was standing with Alexander. Lazarus was there.

Simon said, "Come, son, come now, with us. I will tell you again the story of Joseph, the prisoner who became a king… It is time now"

Rufus raised his arms to the blue sky in praise to Jesus. He was home. The last sound on earth that he heard was his father's song… gradually swallowed up by a lion's roar…and rescue.

Soli Deo gloria.

EPILOGUE

The Lion
"The great cat kept all the others away."

Rufus never got to see his name written in Paul's letter to the church at Rome. Sister Phoebe was faithful to deliver the letter to John Mark in Rome where he dutifully copied it word for word. As the story goes, Rufus was already with Jesus, in the land of the living, when the letter finally arrived.

There are ancient Roman records that hint at someone named Rufus being thrown to the lions in the year AD 57. It was an unusual execution. Apparently, one massive lion stood by Rufus's lifeless body that day, while the pack slowly circled the victim. The great cat kept all the others away as if to prevent the prisoner from being torn apart. The ancient cryptic reference indicates the beast quickly took the life of Rufus in one crushing blow to his heart, then stood guard over the fallen man until the crowd dispersed.

Paul was beheaded by Nero just a few years later in AD 61. Copies of "Romans" were eventually sent to the various churches throughout Asia Minor. To this day, it remains, perhaps, the best pure doctrinal statement on salvation through the forgiveness and mercy of God.

Forgiveness is truly the foundation of the Christian faith. It was modeled by Christ as he pleaded with his father to forgive the executioners who were nailing him to a Roman cross.

"They don't realize what they are doing," he said. It was on that same cross that the punishment for mankind's sin was atoned for, and we were fully captured by the immeasurable love of God. We were forgiven.

Tradition tells us that little Simone grew up and followed the missionary trail to Britannia that was opened for the gospel by Joseph of Arimathea. She never married but served the church for many years in what is now the United Kingdom. Her mother, Evangeline, joined her after the death of Malchus. They are both buried behind a tiny stone church that has stood for centuries near Aylesbury. There is no known grave belonging to Rufus. He is believed to be buried in the caverns, beneath the streets of Rome.

***

This concludes the story of my brother, Rufus…unless, of course, you believe. For those who do, this story never ends, and you are in it. I, Alexander, am one who now believes. I have seen grace in this life, and I will dwell in absolute grace forever. Thank you, Rufus. Thank you, Jesus.

I Love You, Church
Modern Parables

Loren Paul Decker

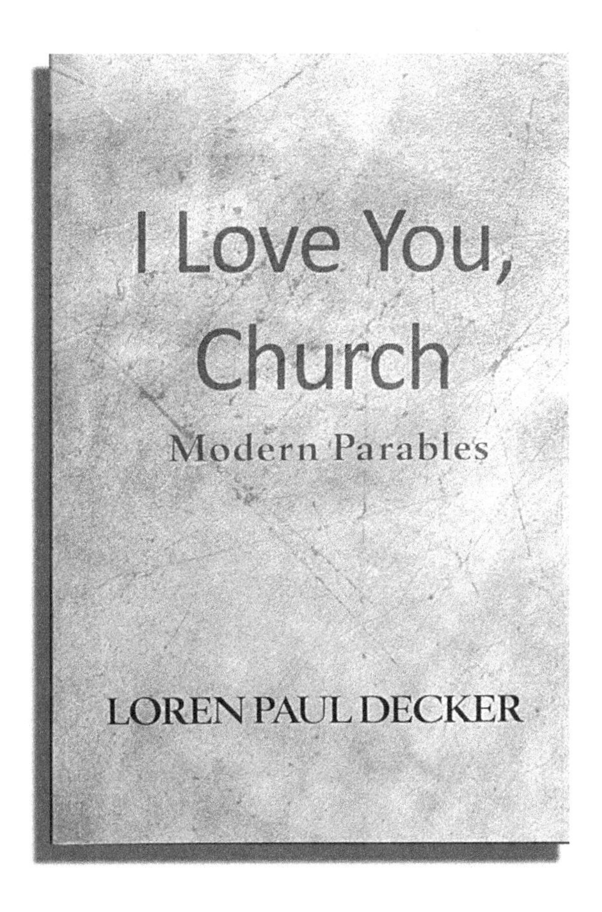

As Jesus once told stories about day-to-day realities like farming and sheep to illustrate the kingdom of God, Pastor Decker now relates tales of grocery stores, car trips, and the darndest things his kids say—all revealing loving messages from the heart of the Father. Many of the firsthand accounts in this book began as sermon illustrations at LifeHouse Church where Loren pastors. Now he shares them with everyone. You will laugh and cry as you follow these stories that point to the deepest truth of all—that we are loved by God.

Soul Chaser

Loren Paul Decker

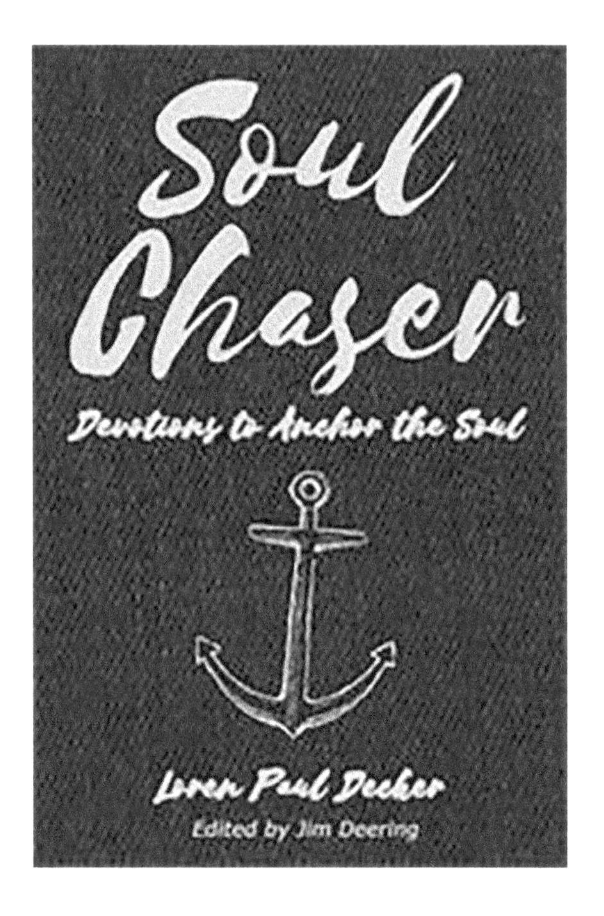

Spiritual growth is just what it says it is. The growth of one's spirit. It stretches your capacity for God. It opens us to experience Him at a soul level. Not just in our brains but in our very beings as well.

This devotional will deepen your love for the One who fashioned your spirit in His likeness. You'll meet interesting characters in this book—Joseph the tin man, an orphaned woman named Lola, a blind young beggar named Timmy Two, and a brokenhearted boy… because of a father's words that couldn't be taken back. Perhaps one of these will catch you.

ABOUT THE AUTHOR

Loren Paul Decker grew up in Massachusetts where he attended Gordon College. After completing his studies there, he entered the world of Christian broadcasting. He spent the next twenty years partnering with Dr. John DeBrine as a producer and a host of the nationally syndicated program *Songtime USA*.

He left radio and entered the pastorate in 1997 becoming the first full-time minister of the historic First Baptist Church in Middleboro, Massachusetts. He eventually moved across town and became the senior pastor of LifeHouse Church in 2009.

Loren is happily married to Amanda Decker. Their children are a source of joy to them both. *Rufus* is his third book.

CPSIA information can be obtained
at www.ICGtesting.com
Printed in the USA
LVHW090501310721
694023LV00003B/389